INDEPENDENT
LEGIONS
PUBLISHING

Horror Writers
ASSOCIATION
SPECIALTY PRESS AWARD RECIPIENT

MORT CASTLE
KNOWING
WHEN TO DIE

ISBN: 978-88-31959-01-8
Copyright (Edition) ©2018 Independent Legions Publishing
Copyright (Work) 2017©Mort Castle
Editing: Michael Bailey
Cover Art by Wendy Saber Core

TABLE OF CONTENTS

000

MORT CASTLE

KNOWING WHEN TO DIE

*Jane, who has been there
with and for me
throughout every decade
spent in attaining overnight success...*

I AM YOUR NEED

I

August 4, 1962
The Brentwood Section of Los Angeles

Marilyn Monroe lies naked and dying.

You can see it there, at that spot on her forehead where electrolysis permanently removed her widow's peak. Just beneath the skin's surface, a blue-black flower grows.

It is Death.

There is the promise of finality in her every tentative breath, the sporadic sighings, the intimation of ending.

Marilyn Monroe is dying.

I am her death. And I will die, too.

That is, when she dies, I have to assume I will also cease to be. Marilyn Monroe. She was born in the flesh and of the flesh.

Like you.

And I?

I was born of her need. I *am* her need.

II

February 6, 1961
New York

I could not bear it. I could endure no more. I wanted to die.

No, I need *to die.* That is what I thought.

The address of the Lonesome Capitol of the world is East Fifty-

Seventh Street: the Millers' apartment, now my apartment. His typewriter was gone, his Oxford Unabridged was gone, his leather-bound copy of *Madame Bovary*, the first "quality book" he ever bought, his underwear, his Schick electric shaver, the silk tie he wore when he testified before HUAC ... He did not take the picture of me I had given him, the one in which I wear white gloves (hiding my ugly hands, my ugly, ugly, ugly hands) and a hat that Mamie Eisenhower might have worn. I looked "demure" in the picture, he said. I looked regal and contemplative and lovely, he said. I kissed him regally and demurely and even contemplatively, and then I fucked him until his eyes rolled back in his head and he screamed some things none of his characters will *ever* be allowed to say on stage.

I stood at the living room window. Below, the city. (The Asphalt Jungle! The Naked City! Broadway, the busiest and loneliest street in the world! All the clichés of popular culture are true!) It was a perfectly cold, perfect blue-sky February afternoon. You cannot be more alone than that.

It seemed Death was summoning me. My marriages were dead. My marriage to Jim Dougherty, Just Plain Jim, the sweet Irish merchant marine. To the jealous and decent, sweet and hot-tempered Yankee Clipper, my slugger, my Joltin' Joe.

And now, to the New York Jewish Liberal Intellectual, Arthur. I called Arthur *Pops* or *Popsie*. I consider *The Crucible* his best work. He was surprised, you know, that I understood the play so well that anyone as blonde as I could possibly comprehend metaphor and symbol. I got mad when he told me that. I cried. I told him I wasn't stupid. I told him I understood metaphor and symbol, understood better than he, because I goddamned good and goddamned well *was* metaphor and symbol, and the way he looked at me then, the way he looked at me, that clever observing way, I knew the bastard someday would use what I had said in a play.

So I loved Arthur Miller. So Arthur Miller loved me, but, when you realize something like that, no, you cannot stay married to a man.

There were other voices beckoning me, calling me to the Nation of the Dead.

My children. I don't know how many had been scraped out of me, poor little blobs—you have to force yourself to lose track of

8

statistics like that—but all those children died and they cursed me. They cursed my tubes so I could never have sons or daughters. They left behind a dead womb.

The dead call out ...

There, the insane contralto of Della Monroe, dear old Gram, who muttered she smelled strange scents in the house that nobody else could smell: burning silk, fish oil, lye soap, and something she called "the lurid stink of God's black flowers." There were men in wool suits, men with gray hats and well shined shoes; they had to be men from "the Society, The Internal Agency, the Office of Dispatch and Remnants, that's who they were," and they followed her. They sat behind her on street cars, always two seats behind. They held the door when she stepped into a department store. They had accents, but the accents kept changing, French, Spanish, Eastern European ...

You know, it's weird, but if you really try, I bet you can remember everything, everything, no matter how young, and I can remember Gram's lopsided determined smile as she pressed a pillow down on me. I can still summon that wet feather taste. In my nightmares I taste it. I was maybe 14 months old or so when Gram tried to kill me.

Someone stopped her. Mama? That, I can't remember for sure. Maybe I have not tried hard enough. I might need more analysis. It might have been my mother.

Poor Gladys, and sometimes you think she had to be doomed because she was named Gladys (I chose my name, I choose my names, Marilyn Monroe, Zelda Zonk, Journey Evers, but I cannot run away from the what I am!); not all that long after Gram played "Baby Want Pillow," my mother went crazy herself; one day, instead of just looking nervous, with her hands flying this way and that, she sat down and started crying. "I can't, I can't, I just can't ..." She kept saying that and she went off to the asylum and that's where you will find her today.

Family tradition: Gram got packed off to the insane asylum and died there.

(Was the Monroe Madness my inheritance? I've frequently discussed that with my psychiatrists. We talk about "nature and nurture," genetic tendencies, then they prescribe new drugs. I give the Demerol four stars, but fuck that Seconal: leaves you with a cotton brain and the flavor of a day-old Dr. Scholl's corn pad in your mouth. But mostly my therapists want me to talk about fucking. A couple have wanted to do more than talk.)

Oh, and by the way, my movie was dead.

It was/had been called *Something's Got to Give*. I had insisted on a tasteful swimming pool nude scene, so tasteful that tasteful stills had tastefully been carried in the always tasteful *Life* magazine, pictures which tastefully showed my tasteful tits, the top of my tasteful tush-crack (a far cry, don't you think, from such digest-size stroke mags wherein my image used to appear as *Caper, Dizzy Winks,* and *Hotcha Babe!*), but the production was all shut down, boom-thud-boom. Studio lawsuits against me. Countersuits against the studio.

All right, the script was dreck à la dreck. That did not matter. *Some Like It Hot* is the kind of "filmic vehicle" that might have starred Gale Storm with Moe, Larry, and Curly, had they had a better agent, some luck, and the ability to read. As it is, *Hot* was perfect for me: I became a respected *comédienne* (accent it properly, if you please), a "luminous and gifted comic actress with impeccable timing and commanding presence," said Archer Kellbourne in the *New York Times*.

> *Something's Got to Give* could have been my salvation.
> Fuck it. I did not want salvation.
> *Something's got to give and the something is me.*
> Okay. Grandiose, I know. Self-pitying shit.
> Solipsistic.

Does it surprise you that such a word is in my vocabulary? I have, after all, despite its aging, what has been appraised as a "million dollar ass" by no less an authority than Hollywood raconteur and celebrated ass connoisseur Groucho Marx. With an ass you can take to the bank, why, mercy-on-my-Pie-O-My, why ever would you even *need* a brain? Pay attention, *s'il vous plaît* (she said multilingually—which has nothing to do with giving you a blow job): Here are other words I know and can properly use: insouciant, ontological, non-sequitur, dialectic, moribund, phlegmatic, truculent ...

May I not say, "Seurat's pointillism never descends into perfunctory technique or mannerism?" Do you think, "That guy sure knew how to paint real pretty with all those little dots" is the MM style?

Maybe you are right. Maybe I am a dumb blonde. After all, I did fuck Yves Montand. Ah, zee debonair French, so cosmopolitan that it's amazing they've never taken to deodorant.

The hell with it.

The hell with it already.

It was time to die, time to stop concerning myself about what I truly was, and what people thought I was, and …

Fuck it. It was time to die.

My first thought was to step out onto the ledge, to take that deepest of breaths as I sucked in clean winter air, to look up at the sky and to see it with the utmost clarity and then to leap.

Step out onto the ledge …

My god, that would be like a scene from *I Love Lucy.* "Loo-seeee, choo get back in *la casa muy pronto!* You got some 'splainin' to do."

I wanted to die.

I did not want to be ridiculous.

So I opened the huge living room window as wide as possible. And then I backed up.

I would run and hurl myself out. A swan dive (just like Esther Williams—to her credit, she never attempted to act—or think), only *sans* water. I had heard that jumpers lost consciousness before they landed and there was an appeal in that.

I clenched my fists.

I licked my lips. They were dry and rough. My mouth felt cottony. Nembutal and Dom Pérignon and chloral hydrate, an always interesting aftertaste.

I could hear my heart beat but not feel it. That was curious, I thought.

And then I ran but it was not so much running as floating, and I didn't know if I could really do it, if I had the force of will to kill myself.

Then just before the jump, I looked down, and there was someone out there, someone on the sidewalk, someone looking up at me—and I knew him; I could see his face, despite the distance, and I knew him even though I did not know who he was—Daddy?

(—you have had the feeling, haven't you, maybe just once in your life, but you have experienced it and so this is not a delusion of mine or a paradox for you, is it?)

—and I said, "N-No— No."

(I stuttered as a child. Sometimes, even though I am now all grown up, I still do.)

I changed my mind.

I made a rational decision: I did not have to die. I was meant to live. I was a survivor.

But momentum or destiny or something worse carried me on, carried me toward the cold and the window and then I thrust my arms out, locking my elbows, and the heels of my hands smashed hard against the window sill and the shock went all the way up into my teeth and I went reeling backward.

I did not die.

A day later, I checked myself into the Payne Whitney Psychiatric Clinic at New York Hospital, where I was classified as suicidal, which was neo-Jungian, post-Freudian, Harry Stack Fucking Sullivan bullshit.

Fuck that, Freddy.

Marilyn Monroe is a survivor.

III

If it can be said that I am *capable* of surprise, I am often surprised by all that I know—and by all that I do not know:

For example, I can intelligently discuss existentialism, possibly win an argument with Jean-Paul Sartre himself, if need be. (Existence before essence, yes—albeit not in *my* case.) Let the subject turn to the aesthetics of cinematography, and I will explain the importance of the Eisenstein montage and the Gance panorama. Shall we focus on the universal themes of Osip Mandelstam's modernist poetry or the immensity of suffering in Picasso's "Guernica" or the myriad subtleties of vocal shading in the performances of June Christie?

Marilyn needed me to be smart, to be intellectual and artistic. You were no dunce, Marilyn, no dim-bulb bimbo, no sack-ready starlet with a VACANCY sign on her forehead and HOT TO TROT on her round heels. You needed intellect and that is what I became (in part!) and what I am.

I am your need.

Yet I have no idea how to write a check. That is because you had others to take care of that. On an afternoon kiddy TV show, I heard the word *hygrometer*; I have no concept of what it is, what it does, why it is needed, any more than do you. You thought Sukarno was the president of India, not Indonesia; you had no idea of the history, the culture, or even the location of either country and so, neither do I.

Yet you were, in your way, *political* and so I had to be "political." I guess you would have to call me a New Frontier Democrat. Here I always aver, Marilyn, to your reasoning:

Jack is a damned clever politician and progressive thinker and not such a bad lay, say a six or seven, but he's more in love with himself than he could ever be with anyone else (poor Jackie, poor, poor Jackie), or with the country for that matter and Bobby Kennedy is a good man, usually, even if being Catholic has made him nuttier than most Catholics, and he is so smart that he doesn't feel threatened by a smart woman and so it's good to talk to him and he is a good politician and maybe he will be able to help people the way he wants and maybe Jack can help him, if Jack's ego will permit, and you know what is really nice is that he really does love his wife and kids, so no matter how bad he wants to put it to Marilyn! Monroe! and wants to even more because Big Brother has greased the gears, no matter what, Bobby probably won't do it—and you do have to respect a man who won't fuck you ...

Here is what else I know, Marilyn.

You needed me.

And when the need was powerful enough, when it was pure ferocity of need, then, like magic, like dream, like aneurism or lottery, like the roll of the dice, the whirl of the Great Mandela.

I am.

With no burden or pride of personal history, with no more clue to my beginnings than had any flea-bite scratching caveman, there I am!

I am
your need
I AM

IV

September 4, 1958
Early afternoon

San Diego is the best city in California and perhaps in the United States. The weather is always so near to perfect that you do not think at all about the weather. The youth are golden and smell of sea water and lotions and if you see one of them frowning it is noteworthy. Old cars have no rust, no wrinkles, no dents, nor do old people. Dos Picos Park is the favorite park of San Diego's residents. The oak trees are majestic as only oaks can be and the shadows cast by their limbs are not frightening. And there are the ducks waiting in the pond. The ducks like visitors.

She liked being here, squatting at the water's edge, tossing oyster crackers to the appreciative ducks. She should have been in makeup and costume, should have been on the set at Coronado Beach, but she had decided to be difficult, a star turn and how do you like it, you assholes. She could not stand to be with Mr. Billy Wilder, a certified prick (figuratively speaking) but without the sensitivity of a prick (literally speaking); and she couldn't stand to be with Curtis, who told her, "The script says I kiss you, but kissing you is like kissing Hitler."

Curtis probably would delight in kissing Hitler. The uniform and the leather boots and all. Ooh, and that riding crop ... Curtis definitely thought he could out-beautiful her. Fucking fake would look like a mummified drag queen when he got old—and that wasn't in the least ironic because ...

Oh, God, she was so afraid, she was so afraid. The mind was going: *Tilt! That's all, Folks! Right into the Mad Mad Monroe Maelstrom.*

"It's me, Sugar." That was her part, her only line, for yesterday's scene. "It's me, Sugar." Sugar Kane, ukulele-strumming flapper; that is your role, that's who you become this time.

Here is the *Reader's Digest Condensed* version of what she said:

I— i-it's sugar, me.
Sugar me
... ...

It is I! Cigar
It's just me, sugar pie.
It's just fucking sugar shit fuck fuck ...

It required 37 fucking takes for her to say, "It's me, Sugar." 37 takes to synch brain with mouth to get out words that Lassie could have managed with one hand-cue from trainer Rudd Weatherwax and the promise of two Gaines biscuits.

And there was Billy Wilder, looking like he hadn't had a dump in three weeks and had no hope for the future, and Mr. Tony "I Feel Pretty" Curtis throwing his hands in the air.

She had to get away, had to, had to be alone?

—did not want to be alone, so alone—

Incognito time. Easy, surprisingly easy. Forget Max Factor and Maybelline. Slip on the kind of dark glasses that sell three for a dollar at the Texaco station and tie a scarf over the blondeness, and a far too big UCLA sweatshirt (Tits? Tits? In this potato sack?) and the kind of shapeless skirt that would embarrass a Jehovah's Witness, and you disappear, you become nobody—

—I'm nobody. Who are you?

I'm nobody but I need to be somebody and I need to show them show them all that I am somebody and I need to be loved and need to be somebody need to be somebody's and I need and I need and I need—

V

I take her elbow, feel that tremoring within like a too tightly wound clock spring. She is not surprised that I am here.

I am her need, corporeal, need now made manifest, though I have always been with her.

We sit on a bench. "The crackers," she says. "Whenever I go to a restaurant, I always take the crackers for the ducks. I love animals."

I know.

I know she needs to tell me about her love for animals, needs me to hear about this goodness in her.

"I've always loved animals."

I know.

"Want to hear a funny story?"

She needs me to hear a funny story, needs to remind herself of a time when her life could be safely compartmentalized in funny little stories, mundane events no larger than life and nothing in the least crazy.

"My first husband, Jim; it was when we were first married. We went off on this weekend. He had friends near Van Nuys and they had this small farm. They called it a ranch 'cause everything's a ranch in California, but it really was a farm.

"So we went out to their farm and they were our age—well, Jim's age, he was five years older than me, you know—and we played gin rummy and danced to the radio. We were drinking Blatz beer. I remember that 'cause it was the sponsor of the radio remote we were listening to, *Live from the Congress Hotel in Chicago*, with Eddy Howard and his orchestra.

"Anyway, then we went off to bed and it had started to rain and, next thing I knew, I heard a calf outside; it was mooing, you know, and it was so lonely sounding ...

"I told Jim we had to get it, had to take it out to the barn.

"He laughed at me.

"I never minded when Jim laughed at me. If that fuckface Tony Curtis laughs at me, if that fly boy even dares, I'll pull his panties up around his neck and strangle him, but I *liked* it when Jim laughed at me.

"'Babe,' he said, 'don't worry about that calf. Little guy will be all right. He's covered in leather.'"

Marilyn was silent.

She thought she needed silence.

But I knew otherwise, of course, because I was her need. She had to tell me—

—*the worst, the most tragic and horrible animal story she knew. She needed to tell me the story—*

"No."

No?

I am her need and a need can be patient, patient but insistent. She had no choice, not really: One must acquiesce to need, always, always.

She began to cry then.

So many tears, Marilyn, so many tears so many times.

Then she said, "I had a dog once. Cinders. I was in a foster home then. Cinders was only a puppy, a very sweet puppy, and funny, and like puppies do, Cinders barked a lot. A neighbor got mad about it, just really furious and what he did, I saw it, he picked up this hoe and he chopped Cinders in half. I saw it."

Again, a silence. A needed silence.

"Maybe it was then I started to go crazy."

VI

August 4, 1962
The Brentwood Section of Los Angeles

Marilyn Monroe is dying.

Her diaphragm has quit working and her breathing is now all from the stomach. The color of her aureoles is fading. I touch her hand, then her wrist. I can find her pulse but only with difficulty, regular but slow, so very slow and thin. There is a tranquility to her flesh that morticians strive for and never achieve.

She is dying because she needs to die.

And, curious, so curious, I do not understand it but I feel no abatement of my selfness, no ebbing away of my consciousness.

I who have never been alive feel no less alive than ... than previously.

I am her need.

And to myself I am becoming an enigma.

V

You need to hear about the sex, don't you?

I know what you need. After all, she fascinates you, compels your ever-so-avid interest, Mr. and Mrs. Main Street America:

—you, regular fellas at the Tip Top Lounge ... with the wisdom imparted by the old after-work boilermaker, you know you'd have her wailing once you gave her the old Jack Hammer John.

—you, Lutheran housewives in Michigan who have begun to get the hint from her this hyperbolic persona that is MM: women are supposed to like it, too.

—you, the thirteen-year-old horn rimmed smart boy. You are a whiz with the slide rule, but now you are discovering there's something about Marilyn Monroe's gyrating buttocks that puts lead in the little pencil.

—you, the desperate nineteen-year, selling ribbons at Woolworth's, just a little orthodonture shy of being beautiful, dreaming of love, dreaming of Hollywood, dreaming of magic.

All of you, all of you, I understand your need. How can I not?

So, addressing the topic of Marilyn Monroe's womanhood, I speak with a degree of expertise, a PhD, if you will.

Marilyn Monroe not infrequently needed fucking and I am her need.

And so, on occasion, I fucked her the way she needed to be fucked, fucked her hard and then harder, knowing she relished the sensation at the spot just above her anus where the testicles go slap-slap-slap, the hot juices flowing along mounds and fissures, fucked her with her hips doing the comma-wriggle bump and pump, fucked her with the exact length and girth and temperature of cock her need demanded at that particular time for that particular fuck, fucked her saying all the amorous vulgarities she needed to hear: *You beautiful, wild bitch, you hot cunt, you whore, you sweet pussy, you ...*

I fucked her.

And so many times, when she came (came because she needed to come), she cried and she cried out, "Daddy!"

I am her need.

she needed daddy and she needed fucking and she needed home and she needed sanity and she needed respect and she needed dignity and she needed

she needed she was a sucking vacuum of need an endless deep need at the core of the universe she was

she needed limits and laughter and kindness and concern and gentleness and daddy oh god she needed daddy she needed she needed she needed love she needed love she needed love she needed love she needed she needed she was

All Need. All Consuming Need.

and i am

VI

August 4, 1962
The Brentwood Section of Los Angeles

I am often surprised by all that I know—and by all that I do not know.

I have told you that, haven't I? I must be telling you again because it is something you need to know.

I heard the wet rattle within the V-juncture of throat and collar bone. It was a death rattle. I had never heard it before (how could I?) but I knew its significance.

Marilyn Monroe was dying.

She would die and I would be no more.

Then I was startled; that's what it was. I was *startled* at the sudden slow movement, as her head lolled on the pillow, and white-tinged mucus bubbled at the parched corner of her mouth.

She sat up. It was melodramatic but no less comic and grotesque. Her eyes sought focus and found it.

She looked at me. She smiled.

"No," she said. "Not this time. Not ever. No."

I am her need. I have always been her need.

"No. Fuck this," she said. "I can ..."

I understood her, understood her even when she did not understand herself.

Lie down now, I told her. You need to die.

"No ..."

I am your need.

Marilyn Monroe lies naked and Marilyn Monroe lies dead.

And I made her die.

VII

August 4, 1962
The Brentwood Section of Los Angeles

Marilyn Monroe is dead.

Her heart has stopped. Her blood no longer circulates. Lividity discolors and distorts her features. You might no longer know who she is.

She isn't. Marilyn Monroe is defunct. (That is a literary allusion: e.e. cummings. She needed literary allusions.)

Marilyn Monroe is dead.

And I?

VIII

A mystery, if you need a mystery.

I am here.

Marilyn Monroe is gone and I am here.

And if I do not understand, then, very well, that is the way of it, I suppose, I assume, I would think, I do surmise: who attains full understanding? Jesus, Buddha, Mohammed, Joseph Smith, Mary Baker Eddy, Norman Vincent Peale, Bishop Fulton Sheen ...

But I think I am beginning to realize, to know:

you

you are alone in a lonely night and you cannot bear the sound of your own heart cannot tolerate the touch of your mocking breath as it leaves your nostrils to brush your upper lip and the weight of your existence offends you

you

you are at the city's busiest intersection on this busy day and the sunlight that pours down is weighted and cutting and you feel it slice away the flesh slice away all that protects and keeps you hidden

you

you have children and they hate you and you hate them

you are watched all the time watched by secretive men who know what uncle did and know how dirty you are and though they are biding their time for now they will act they will

you are lies covered over with lies covered over with lies and all covering the truth the terrible impossible unendurable truth

you are fifty-two years old and you still cry for daddy you have no satisfactions

you have no joy

you (all of you) you are unloved and you are unlovable and you are cursed (all of you forever children alone in the dark) and you cannot try cannot dare cannot hope (all of you the forever lost

the forever lonely) and you cannot hope and you need you need
you need
    and you need
    you need death
    and
    I am
    your need

THE DOCTOR, THE KID,
AND THE GHOSTS IN THE LAKE

I

INDIAN CAMP, PART ONE

*Many Years Ago
in the Ojibway Camp
at Ghost Lake, Michigan*

Hey-aye-hey!
Hey, Doc. Hey, kid.
Kid get big. Ha! Kid play moccasin game plenty much?
Ah, Doc bring Great Spirit! Cyrus Noble whiskey. Strong medicine! Doc friend of Indian.
Kid? Oh. You bet ghosts in lake. Why you think call it Ghost Lake? No bullshit. Go where moon float on water. Look down. See plenty ghosts, damn right.
How get there?
Hey-aye-yah! Red man tell story. True stuff. No bullshit. More Cyrus Noble. Strong medicine, damn right. Indian got plenty stories for white man.
Long ago two braves fight for pretty woman. Name Winona. Braves fight on shore. Winona in canoe in lake. Braves fight with knives.
Blood flyin'. Winona clap hands. Say, "Ooh. Ah!" Have one damn fine time, no bullshit.
Braves cut each other all to hell. Plenty blood.
"Ooh!" say Winona.
Then big surprise!

22

Neebanaw grab her! Neebanaw King Spirit of Lake.
Neebanaw drag her down.
Ghost? Hey, damn right Winona ghost.
Winona *lonely* ghost.
Winona want sister ghosts.
Bitch ghosts just like her.
Tribe have bitch woman, man have bitch wife, bitch
daughter. *Hey-aye-hey*, you just take bitch in canoe
and send her to Neebanaw and Winona!
Plenty ghosts in lake. Damn right.
Hey-aye-yah!

– Gilby Edwards

II

NOBODY EVER DIES

1961
Mayo Clinic
Rochester, Minnesota

For many years, people had often called him "Papa" or "Mr.
Papa" or "Señor Papa," and he often called himself in this way,
although not all his children called him so, but now it was 1961
and he was sixty-one and in 1961 you were an old man, a
"Papa"—*verdad!*—if you were sixty-one years old. He said, "The
address, I can remember it. We lived there in 1923 and 1924. The
first wife and I. In Paris. It was good then. Good wife for me
then." He lowered his head. "Long time ago good."

He looked sad and confused, but more confused than sad. He
also looked a little foolish because on his steel-rimmed eyeglasses
was a clumsily wrapped and dirty wad of white adhesive tape on
the nose-piece that he'd put there so the glasses did not cut into
his flesh. He wore a much-washed flannel shirt, loose corduroy
trousers, two pairs of white socks because his feet often were
cold, even though he sweated a great deal, and leather bedroom
slippers he had bought eleven years ago at Abercrombie and
Fitch. Over this, he had on a red Italian robe he called "The
Pasha's Imperial dressing gown" for reasons he could not recall

and this also made him seem old.

"Now no good," he said.

"No good?" the psychiatrist said. He was quite a modern psychiatrist, so sometimes he was non-directive. "Your present life …"

The old man ignored the non-directiveness. He was quite a famous writer who had written many famous novels and stories. One of them was about an old man and a great fish and some critics said it was a religious story. It was a parable. Jesus wasn't the only one who could make parables. That story, the parable, appeared in a magazine that sold many millions of copies. Motion pictures had been made of that story and others of his stories. Usually, the movies were not very good, but they brought in very good money, so he could sail his boat, a diesel-powered, thirty-eight-footer christened *El Señor Santiago*, so he could go where he pleased in the world, and shoot big game in Africa, and pay considerable alimony, and the movies, even though no good, helped make him famous even to people who did not read his books or any books at all for that matter. Some critics of influence had pronounced him the best living American writer and sometimes he boasted publicly, saying much the same thing. Sometimes he thought it funny that he could be the best living American writer, making very good money and being so famous, and still be so profoundly sad.

"No, I cannot remember," the old man said. He shrugged, confused and sad. "It feels strange, you know. My address in 1923 was 54 rue du Corporal Lemoins. I remember that. I can't remember my present address. I cannot remember my present wife's name. My present wife, I remember she's a nice person. Solid and healthy and a real trooper. She is a good shot. I think she came to see me yesterday."

"It is simple, really, It is the electroshock," the psychiatrist said.

"Simple," the old man agreed. It was, really. For a brief time, your soul left your body; he understood that. It had happened to him before: he thought it had happened when he was a boy, and he knew it had happened when he was a man in the wars. Your soul goes away for a while and then your soul returns. Most of it, anyway.

The psychiatrist continued, "Your memory will come back

after a while once you have completed the treatments."

"Memories do that," the old man said. "They come back. Just like ghosts."

"I wouldn't worry about it if I were you," the psychiatrist said.

"Well, then," the old man said. "Well, good. Nothing to worry about. No, no. Certainly I won't worry about it." He looked embarrassed. "I don't remember your name, either. You are my present psychiatrist?"

The psychiatrist smiled. He did not smile well because his lips were thin and his eyes were as cold as a trout's. But he did look intelligent.

"Dr. Koeller."

"Dr. Koeller," the old man said and nodded. "And are you a Catholic? I do remember that, that I asked that my present psychiatrist be a Catholic."

"Yes. I am a Catholic and a psychiatrist."

"Better if you were Italian," the old man said, dubiously. "Or a Spaniard."

"An Italian or Spanish Catholic is preferable?" Dr. Koeller said, non-directively.

"Yes, yes," the old man said. "They are deeply and truly Catholic. You can see their faith."

"I believe in the Holy Ghost, the Holy Catholic Church, the communion of saints, the forgiveness of sins, the resurrection of the body, and life everlasting," Dr. Koeller said.

The old man said, "Nobody ever dies."

"Here." Dr. Koeller leaned forward. "See my faith." He crossed himself very nicely. It was natural and not perfunctory. It made the old man feel better. Dr. Koeller said, "I believe in the Father, in the Son, and in the Holy Ghost."

"Father," the old man said and nodded. "Son." He nodded.

Then he said, "Ghost."

Señor Papa licked his lips. The medicine for his depression made his mouth and lips quite dry. He wanted a rum punch or a daiquiri. "Ghosts," he said. "I believe in ghosts."

"Tell me," Dr. Koeller said. "Tell me about that."

"Tell me a story, Papa," the old man said. He was teasing the Catholic psychiatrist, but for a moment his expression showed that he, like all sentimental and tough men, could be cruel and a liar. "That is what the world demands of me."

"Is it?"

"Yes. No complaints. Demand it of myself. Long time ago, Papa newspaperman. Heap good un. Papa write-um truth. Now Papa make-um fiction. Make-um fables, fantasies. Make-um myths and allegories. Make-um parables." He paused, then tried to look cagey. "Catholic doctor, do you know the difference between writing the truth and writing fiction?"

"No, I don't," Dr. Koeller said.

"Shit. Me, either!" The old man said and laughed. "When it is true, it is *true!*—the old man snapped his fingers—"It is a truth that is truer than true." He tipped his head. He would have looked cunning or even dangerous had there not been dirty adhesive tape on his nose. "How is that, then, Dr. Koeller? Lies reveal truth! Is that a paradox for you?"

"No."

"Don't you have to deal with paradoxes? My Catholic psychiatrist, can you reconcile Freud and Jesus?"

"I have no need to. There is no argument between them. They get along just fine.

Both confront and proclaim the same thing."

"And that is?"

"Truth."

The old man laughed, a very natural hearty laugh. It sounded healthy, like the laugh of a drunken young man. "Good! That is very good! I think I would like to sit and drink with you. I think I might even like to fight with you. I think after drinking and fighting we might be friends. We could tell each other ..."

Dr. Koeller quickly said, "The truth. Would you like to tell me that, Señor Papa?"

"Yes," the old man said.

"I will tell you a story."

III

FATHERS AND SONS

1935
On the Way to Michigan

You feel it on the back of your neck. In the way your scalp tightens. And just like that, you know: you are being watched.

Adam Nichols felt that. He had felt it for some time. Behind them, there are eyes.

The eyes had been watching for a while.

The eyes were The Doctor's eyes.

Toby said, "How is it, Papa?" Toby did not know about the eyes behind them.

"What's that?"

Toby had asked him something he'd missed. "An elephant. Is it like killing a man?"

"No," Adam Nichols said. "You do not need much of a gun to kill a man. Sometimes a man will die from a little wound that would not kill a rabbit. To kill an elephant, you need a big gun. Best I've had was the re-chambered Springfield '03. It had a kick as big as an elephant. It did the job."

The first shot drops the elephant after he has run only a minute or so. They find him easily. He is on his side. There is blood on his flank. The elephant could rise up and attack, but Adam doesn't care because this is his first elephant, this is a giant's death, and he has to be close to it if he is ever to understand. He looks into the elephant's eye with its impossibly long lashes and it seems that the eye is the most alive thing he has ever seen and that he himself is now entering a realm of loneliness that he must walk the rest of his life.

Then he shoots the elephant right in the ear-hole and when the bullet does what bullets do and the message comes to the elephant that it no longer lives, that it will no longer feel the earth shake beneath its great feet, that it will no longer raise its trunk to sample the breeze and its myriad scents, when the elephant gives up the ghost and all its great elephant spirit is fled to the Great Nothing, gone to that which is Naught, it lies a wrinkled heap without dignity: a hugeness of Death. There is nothing terrifying to it any longer.

"I think I would like to go to Africa."

"I think you would like it."

"Papa, would I be afraid?"

"No, I don't think so."

"I would hate to be afraid."

"I will be with you and teach you not to be afraid."

"You will take me to Africa?"

"Yes."

"All right. I will like that. Did your father take you to Africa?"

"No."

"Will you take my mother?"

"I think I would like to. But I don't think she would want to go with me. Not now. Maybe once, but not now."

"But I would be going!"

"Yes."

Adam slowed for a curve. He was cautious on curves with this car. The La Salle had plenty of power but felt wrong on turns, the wheel off and stiff in his hands. Back in Arkansas, garaged in town, was a 1929 Ford roadster with a familiar dented fender, and the smell of his hands on the steering wheel, a car that suited him quite well, but Adam Nichols was a successful writer and it just would *not* do, said present wife, for him to drive such a proletarian motor car, certainly would not, agreed Mother Adeline (that bitch), and so, because he sought to please present wife and that bitch, he was driving a powerful, in-line eight La Salle sedan ($1,700 goddamn it! $1,700!) that smelled too new to be real and was about as long as a tennis court and about as responsive.

He looked over. Toby's head was turned away from him. On the trip, Toby had sometimes talked about his mother and then abruptly stopped talking as though talking about his mother confused him. Toby was Adam Nichols's first son. Adam thought he was a good boy, quite likely. He did not know him that well. Toby had come into the world via Adam Nichols's first wife in Paris. When Toby had been an infant, in a long ago false spring in Paris, their gray and white six-toed cat, Mr. Pickle, had slept protectively in the boy's crib. Then Adam Nichols and first wife got a divorce and wife got Toby and Mr. Pickle and alimony. Mr. Pickle had been a very nice cat.

Now Adam Nichols was taking Toby, his son, so he could teach him things fathers teach sons. How to catch grasshoppers for bait when they are still wet with dew and cannot jump away. How to sense the right moment to shoot when you hunt quail. How to cook trout in bacon grease over a fire. How to make a bed of hemlock branches and a blanket. How to fish from the shore so your shadow did not warn the fish away. These were the things fathers taught sons and for which sons were grateful all their lives, as Adam Nichols was, having learned these things from his father, The Doctor.

There were other things for which he was not grateful. Some of those things that The Doctor had taught him made him pity his father and some made him despise him. One of the things The Doctor had taught him was a saying: "A man can be destroyed but not defeated." The Doctor also used to say, "A man can be defeated but not destroyed." The Doctor had yet another saying, "A man can be destroyed and defeated so fuck it and let's have a drink."

Adam Nichols thought about The Doctor. He thought about that which was good about him and that which was sad. He made himself not think about other things.

Adam Nichols smiled. He wondered if he smiled for the benefit of the eyes in the back seat. He knew he was not smiling a "rueful" smile. No one ever truly smiled ruefully or any such a damned thing. The *rueful smile* and the *happy thought* and such like were the clichés of bad writers who wrote for the pulps and would never understand that a smile was a smile was a smile and a thought was a thought was a thought, and that was that.

Adam Nichols checked the rearview mirror. Now it was no longer just the eyes he could see. Earlier, there had been only the eyes. Now he had another passenger: The Doctor.

His father rode in back. His father wasn't doing anything or saying anything. He was not asleep. The Doctor, his father, Chadbourne Nichols, MD, was dead, had been so for a pretty long time, and so, it could more properly be said that the ghost of Dr. Nichols occupied the La Salle's backseat.

—Your father's ghost was with you?
—True gen.
—That did not scare you?

29

—Nah, after all, he was dead. Dead can't do much, I
guess. Killed himself, The Doctor, you see.
Besides, my good Catholic psychiatrist, we've all got
ghosts with us, don't we?
And you know, I just did not scare all that much. Not
then.

Before Adam Nichols went to war, back then, maybe he used
to scare, but then he had been blown up and felt his soul leave
his body and return to it, and then, sometime after that, he had
carried a dead man on his shoulders, talking to him and quite
clearly hearing him answer and making good sense of it, while his
boots filled with a heavy slush of mud and his own blood. You
don't scare much after your soul has exited and returned,
roundtrip, *lalala,* and after you've chewed the fat and talked all
flap-a-dap with a dead man. Sometimes your mind, well, it goes
lalala, tickity-tick, like an out-of-control flywheel in a clock, but
you don't scare ...

And how could it surprise Adam Nichols that The Doctor's
ghost was with them? The cabin up in Michigan had been his
father's favorite spot on Earth. It was just so pretty; it was just so
goddamn pretty is what it was.

And it was ghost country.

"Papa?"

Toby was back. Maybe he'd talk about his mother and maybe
he wouldn't.

"Hmm?" If you are a father, you say *Hmm* quite often. You
learn to cock an eyebrow. It's better if you smoke a pipe. He did
not smoke a pipe. He smoked cigars, sometimes, when he was in
Cuba, where a man who did not smoke cigars was socially
offensive and probably *maricon.*

"What is it, Toby?"

"Will we see any Indians there, up in Michigan?"

"I don't know," he said. "Maybe. Probably not, though. I think
most of them, the Indians ... The Indians moved away."

Gone, how could they be gone?

*The Indians were real now. They were made real in his mind
by the boy asking and by his memory which he could no more
control than he could the rising of the sun. Gilby Edwards. Prudy.
He could smell the sweet and biting smoky smell and the tired,*

too often washed flannel, and the whiskey. That is what his Indians and his father's Indians smelled like. And smelling the Indians, they became more real than present wife and this son he did not know. He remembered the totally silent, pigeon-toed way the Indians walked. He remembered how they laughed. Indians do not laugh much, ordinarily. Not in the way a white man would call laughing. But once you heard an Indian laugh, you never forget how it was.

"Aren't there any Indians left, Dad?"

Adam Nichols glanced into the mirror that showed what was behind them. The Doctor—his father's ghost—was smiling with his eyes. His father liked Indians. He understood a little of their sorrow. Perhaps he understood it better than his own.

Indians had taught them both quite a lot, father and son.

"Maybe some. Maybe ghost Indians."

Toby laughed.

Toby liked the little tick of fear it gave him to think about ghost Indians.

IV

INDIAN CAMP, PART TWO

*Many Years Ago
in the Ojibway Camp
at Ghost Lake, Michigan*

Hey-aye-hey!
What are the ghosts like?
Nah, kid. Nah. That white man's question! They like nothin'. Ghosts in lake just ghosts. Jiibay. Spirit. Red man, white man, we all got spirit inside. Ghost, that your spirit. You know, Jiibay.
Soul? White preacher talk. Soul go to heaven. Wave bye-bye. Ha! Jesus dance cakewalk. Heap plenty bullshit.
Ghost like ... When you kid, spirit, ah, spirit go free in the night. Fly anywhere. See everything. *Hey-aye-yah!*

Long before White Man, First Ojibway boy travel in spirit through the Four Colors over the Earth. Fly to Moon. Look down. See everything. Everything good and everything bad. See everyone. Everyone good and everyone bad.

See Seven Grandfathers of the All the Nations in Sacred Sweat Lodge. See Comet, *ishkode*, burn across sky. See raven, *rgaagaagi*, pick out eyes of dead Rabbit. See black serpent Kena'beek twist in talon of Keneu' the great war-eagle. See men, *inini* steal horses, steal clothes, steal wives. See fish, *giigoonh*, leap from lake and see bullfrog, *dende*, take piss in pond.

First Ojibway boy see everything.

Kid know. You know, right? *Hey-aye-hey!*

Damn right kid know. You born, you know.

Then you grow up. Still got jiibay spirit but feet heavy. Feet stuck on Earth. Spirit trapped deep in body. Spirit trapped on Earth. No can fly.

Worse for ghost. Jiibay got no body but ghost cannot go to Chief Chibiabos in the Land of Spirits. Jiibay go nowhere. Must stay here.

Red man, white man, ghost, everyone remember flying free in night. Everyone remember and everyone sad.

Cyrus Noble Whiskey good medicine for sad man.

Jiibay? Ha, nothin' for ghosts. No medicine.

Ghosts heap plenty fucked up.

– Gilby Edwards

V

THE DOCTOR AND THE DOCTOR'S WIFE

Many Years Ago
Ghost Lake, Michigan

In the early afternoon, Adam Nichols knew there would be trouble. He and his father sat on the front steps of the cottage.

The Doctor had a bottle of Cyrus Noble whiskey and from time to time sipped from the tin cup he used when they went camping. There was no breeze so you could not smell the lake. The sun was bright.

Just within, in the front parlor she called the "Salon," Mother Adeline was playing the Chopin Études. The Études were difficult. Mother Adeline played beautifully. Mother Adeline's touch was very delicate and very sure. She had to be exceptionally angry.

The Doctor said loudly, "What I wish is I had a harmonica. A good, ten-cent Hohner Marine Band mouth harp. I would play "Camptown Races." 'Do-dah, do-dah, five miles long. Do-dah-do-dah-DAY!' I would play it loud and at least 100 times. That is what I would do."

The Doctor was sweating and his face was red.

Then he said, somewhat louder, "I would play "You're the Flower of My Heart, Sweet Adeline." He cut "Adeline" into three syllables, jagged and precise. His wife thought harmonicas common. She thought songs like "Sweet Adeline" lower than common. She thought such songs vulgar, contemptible, and somehow immoral, as were those people given to listening or singing or playing such songs.

The Doctor and Mother Adeline had had words this morning in their bedroom. They often had words, though seldom in their bedroom, where they seldom found reason to speak to one another. Adam had heard them this morning, even with the door closed. Some of his mother's words he had overheard were "… filthy, a beast and disgusting. You are a heathen."

Mother Adeline sometimes called her husband a "heathen." Several years ago, Mother Adeline had become a Christian Scientist. The Doctor was convinced she did it to spite him and medical science. To spite her, he frequently said one had to have the highest regard and intellectual respect for a religion founded by a morphine addict.

The Études continued through the open window. The tempo did not change. If anything, perhaps the melody grew quieter.

Sunshine came out and leaned against a support column of the porch. She walked like she didn't wish to set the porch boards squeaking. A straw hat shadowed her round face. She was almost ten years old, a darling little girl, and her real name was Marcella Veronica, her mother's choice, which, Sunshine thought, an "astoundingly putrid name."

Sunshine was her pet name, what The Doctor called her. Mother Adeline thought it suited only for a nappy-headed pickaninny. Adam thought her a frequent pest but in a quiet way he loved her more than many boys love their little sisters and he admired her vocabulary for the countless words she knew that he did not know even though he had declared he would be a writer and had already published two stories in his high school literary magazine.

The Doctor said, "Well, well." Like many stern men, he had a core of sentimentality to his nature, which became more sentimental when he drank. "Sunshine." He said her name and you could tell he liked to say it. "*Hey-aye-hey*, Sunshine." He liked to "talk Indian"; Mother Adeline did not approve of The Doctor having Indian friends. She did not approve of Indians. Approval was not her strong suit.

Sunshine said nothing. Adam looked out at the bright glare of sunlight on the lake. He made it a challenge, to look hard at it without squinting. He wanted to see what was really there. He thought if he looked hard enough and long enough he would see just exactly what was and only that, nothing distorted, nothing made bigger or smaller by your thoughts or your vision than it truly was.

Adam Nichols was fifteen years old. It was an age when you feel like you might never understand anything. Sometimes he tried to tell himself he just did not give a damn. Years later, when he did give a damn and had a Catholic wife who gave a damn, he became Catholic.

The Doctor said. "Alas, I have no Hohner Marine Band harmonica. I don't have a washboard or a sweet potato. Or a damn tin whistle or a goddamn Jew's harp." With the thumb and forefinger of his left hand, he circled the neck of the whiskey bottle. "Fortunately," he said, raising his voice as he raised the bottle, "I do have Cyrus Noble." Cyrus Noble Premium Aged Whiskey was the name on the label. He poured his tin cup about half-full.

He sipped. "Ah, now isn't that nice," he said. He sighed. "That is nice. What a nice life! My oh my! Sitting here at my leisure and drinking this aged whiskey and listening to my own sweet Adeline's pretty piano playing, oh, my yes! Goddamn!"

Once, Adam had asked his father why he drank whiskey. His father said it was because whiskey was kind. He said Adam would understand soon enough and Adam thought he didn't understand now, though, and maybe he didn't want to, not ever.

The piano playing ended in the "Salon." The Doctor set his tin cup down hard. The brown whiskey sloshed over the rim. The Doctor applauded. "Bravo! Bravo!"

"Oh, Papa," Sunshine whispered, "don't. Please don't." In some ways, Sunshine was quite a smart little girl.

"Music hath charms! Damn right," The Doctor said, rising. "Come on, Adam. Let's row on over to Indian camp. We'll go see Gilby Edwards, find out how the fishing's going."

The Doctor started to go inside. He had to get his knapsack, he said. Sunshine clutched at his arm, "Papa, please ..."

"*Hey-aye-hey*, Big Chief Doc, maybe him get-um peace pipe smoked," The Doctor said, loudly.

Mother Adeline's voice came out to them. "Do not think I am unaware of your heinous intent!" The music started then, not the Études, but Bach, as delicate as the edge of a newly stropped straight razor.

At the door, The Doctor winked at Adam. "Come on, then," he said. "Let us off to pursue heinous intent."

From inside, Mother Adeline said, "A heathen on his way to the heathen Indians." Her piano playing was exquisitely beautiful.

"Papa?" said Sunshine.

"I'm sorry," The Doctor said. He wagged a finger, telling Adam to "Pick up Mr. Cyrus Noble there, if you please."

"God sees all," Mother Adeline said, her voice quiet, the piano quiet.

"Good," Dr. Nichols said. "I hope he's got a Kodak."

Adam rowed and his rowing was strong and certain and The Doctor drank just enough to keep a little smile on his face.

"This is all right," Dr. Nichols said. "Do you think so, Adam?"

"Yes," Adam said.

The Doctor took a gun out of the knapsack.

"That's Grandpa's gun," Adam said.

"Why, yes," said Dr. Nichols, "the very same. The Patriarch.

Brave Grandfather, a loyal follower of Father Abraham. He carried this weapon during the War Between the States. This is a .32 caliber Smith & Wesson, manufactured in Springfield, Massachusetts."

The Doctor took head-canted aim toward the middle of the lake. "Here comes one of Gilby Edwards's lake ghosts. Bang!" He jerked the gun up as though he had fired it. "Come on, ghosts." He mimed shooting again. "Come on, bitches!"

Adam tried to laugh because he guessed this was supposed to be funny.

The Doctor said to Adam, "You could not hit the broad side of a barn with this pistol if you were inside the barn. You could not hit a bull in the butt were you to crawl up the bull's butt.

"The only goddamned thing you can shoot with this gun is yourself. Just like Grandfather."

Grandfather had pressed the nose of the .32 caliber Smith & Wesson into his ear and blown out some of his brains. In the family, it was said Grandfather had accidentally died cleaning his gun. The Doctor amended that: He said Grandfather had died accidentally cleaning his gun with his ear.

The Doctor squinted as though he were really aiming. The gun jerked in his hand as though it had really been discharged. "Bang!" The Doctor said. "Got the bitch!"

※

"*Hey-aye-hey!*" Gilby Edwards took a drink from the Cyrus Noble bottle. "Son of a bitch," he said, happily. He and Adam sat on the sofa in the yard of Gilby's shanty close to the dock at the Ojibway camp. The sofa's cushions were torn and one end sagged, but it was very comfortable and it was much nicer to sit on something comfortable outdoors instead of indoors so Gilby kept it outside in front and not inside the shanty. The days he worked, Gilby fished and cut logs for a living. He did not work many days. He drank every day. He did not talk all that much but he talked more than most Indians. He wore his hair long and looked like the kind of Indian you would see on a coin.

Gilby took another drink. "White man firewater, sweet son of a bitch," he said.

The Doctor and Prudy Edwards, Gilby's sister, who was

seventeen or a little older, were in the shanty. Even though it was a ways off, sometimes you could hear a little of what was going on in the shanty. It sounded like they were having a good time. Sometimes Prudy or The Doctor laughed or they both laughed together and sometimes Prudy made a sound that was like a laugh but wasn't really a laugh.

What Adam had noticed this summer was that Prudy was quite round in an interesting way. He had noticed that this time, and had realized that, in previous years, he had not noticed the roundness of her. In previous years, he had gone hunting with her and Gilby, sometimes with his father and sometimes not, and he had noticed Prudy was a good shot. He had noticed that her teeth looked very white when she bit into apples. He had noticed she could look into a bright sky with her flat brown eyes wide open and that she had a nice smell like woodsmoke and oranges and a little bit of sweat. He had noticed lots of things about Prudy Edwards in previous years, but he not noticed roundness.

Inside the shanty, Prudy laughed. Adam felt strange. Not bad, but strange. "Say," Adam said, "let me have some of that, why don't you?" He reached for the whiskey bottle.

"Okay with the Doc?"

"Sure, I guess so." Adam said, "You think I ought to go ask him?"

"Nah," Gilby Edwards said and handed him the bottle.

His father had let him drink beer a number of times, but Adam had never drunk whiskey. It tasted hot and mean and made it feel like his throat was pinching shut all the way down the center of his chest to his belly.

Then just like that he felt warm and good and bigger. "Son of a bitch," Adam Nichols said, happily. He took another drink. He felt very good. He thought he was about to understand something very big and important.

It was some time after that that The Doctor came out of the shanty. He was not wearing his shirt. He was hairy across the shoulders.

The Doctor was smiling when he said to Gilby Edwards, "What did you do to him? My boy's got an edge on, Gilby!"

Adam laughed and said, "Son of a bitch."

The Doctor said, "Well," and his smile did not change and Adam did not remember getting to his feet but he was walking toward the shanty with his father alongside him and he was glad that his father was not saying anything and he said nothing and he was aware of the sunlight that filtered down through the gently fluttering leaves overhead and of the shadows and there was a gentle breeze coming off the lake and then he was going into the dark of the shanty.

He could see nothing but he heard his name and it took him a tick of time to realize it was Prudy Edwards saying his name and as that came to him there also came to him an odor that was of his father and of whiskey and of something mysterious and a little frightening.

Then Prudy Edwards called to him again and he went to her.

—And that was your, ah, sexual initiation?
—Damn straight, Dr. Koeller. Damn right, Dr. Koeller. Yer danged tootin' it was, Dr. Koeller.
That was it then. My father brought me to the woman he had been with and then I was with that woman in the way he had been with her and then I was where he had been and that was the way it was then. I think my father loved me very much then. I know I loved my father very much then.
—Well, how was it?
—Aren't you the good Catholic psychiatrist! That's funny. It really is. Are you seeking salient salaciousness of fornication's fine points? Prurient particularities? Did the virgin lad's manly member meet muster? True gen, libidinous Dr. Koeller …

And could you tell him that she was your father's gift and that she did first what no one has ever done better and can you bid memory speak of her good plump brown legs and the good roundness of her tight belly of her fine brown breasts of her round bottom and might you then tell of those well holding arms and well holding legs and of that quick searching tongue and the good taste of mouth and then uncomfortably, tightly, sweetly, wetly, lovely, tightly, achingly, fully, tightly, tightly, finally, unendingly, never-endingly, never-to-endingly, suddenly ended, and it was like your ending it was like your spirit flying free in twilight and then the moment that comes with your sigh when he

knew that nothing not ever again would be so good.
He was right.

VI

THE MOTHER OF A QUEEN

For a day, Mother Adeline was silent. The next day, she did not speak much, but she did play piano: "Swan Lake," which she had often said she loathed for its obviousness and melodrama and other "Slavic qualities." The third day, Mother Adeline was smiling and humming and she fed the birds and sat on the dock with her floppy straw hat shading her face and bare feet in the water and in the early afternoon picked berries and then made a pie and you would think her ever the contented housewife and sometimes she stopped at the piano to play something so delicate and melodic that it required only two fingers of the right hand and two of the left. Oh, my, Mother Adeline seemed ever so cheery, lah-de-dah. Why, boys will be boys, lah-de-dah. Like father, like son, lah-de-dah. They just go off to Indian Camp to do heinous things with savages.

There would be Hell to pay, Adam knew that; he was old enough to realize there always comes a reckoning. What he ought to do maybe was light out. Pack a tent, snitch bacon and flour, and take to the woods in the night, and, in the true first light of morning, keep on traveling. Light out for territories. Didn't he ramble? Canada. The Arctic Circle. Borneo. Africa.

And why in hell hadn't the Doctor lit out? How is it we get trapped?

—Even then, the old man says to the psychiatrist, even then I had the sense we're all bitched.
—Hmm, is the response, non-directive.
—Bitched and that's how it is. You just got to take it and not complain. Man's got to do what a man's got to do, says the old man.
—John Wayne. *High Noon.* Gary Cooper, Dr. Koeller said. You could show you knew and liked movies and still be non-directive.
—Coop's all right. He's my friend, Cooper. Damned

good bird shooter. Good as me. Damned good Catholic. Better than me.

I am going to miss Coop. The Big C. Maybe Coop has got a month. Maybe. Then he's heading for the barn. Should call him but you can't talk to Coop on a goddamn phone. You need to be by a trout stream, drinking a little whiskey and branch water ...

Goddamn, Cooper.

The old man feels his eyes tear up. Too many absent friends. Too many losses. Too many gone missing. The missing won't kill you, though. It's the despair. Too many gone oh our father who art in *pues y nada y pues y nada* hallowed be thy *pues y nada y pues y nada ...*

The old man knows he's talking talk that doesn't mean much but he's also thinking and thinking something that feels as though he might be thinking it for a first time: Maybe The Doctor was trapped because of Sunshine. Could not leave dear little Sunshine girl to Mother Adeline. Mother Adeline ate her young.

Or perhaps it is that The Doctor was no less trapped because of me ...

And now, it is after Mother Adeline's good dinner, and they are all of them in the parlor, the light soft and dusty with sunset more than two hours off. And Adam beneath the window, curve of back against the wall, with *Gallagher and Other Stories*, the adventures of a boy detective, a book he first read when he was much younger but still returns to frequently because Richard Harding Davis is such a crackerjack writer. And Mother Adeline reading Mrs. Mary Baker Eddy's *Science and Health with Key to the Scriptures*, and The Doctor and his *Sporting News*, clucking his tongue over "Frank Gotch retiring but damn, maybe it is time," and Sunshine on the floor with paper and colored pencils, drawing a horse, her tongue just at the corner of her mouth, concentrating, lost in swirls and lines.

Sunshine is happy.

Mother Adeline cannot abide happiness.

"Marcella Veronica," Mother Adeline says, "I think I would like to hear you play Schumann, the "Scenes from Childhood." You play it well, dear. Yes, that would be quite pleasant."

"Oh," says Sunshine, losing her concentration. "Not now."

Oh, Jesus, Adam thinks, and The Doctor's *Sporting News* makes a fold-crinkling sound. It feels as if all the air has been sucked out of the room.

Mother Adeline says, "Excuse me? Pardon me? Excuse me?"

"We ..." Sunshine says, but look at her and you can see she knows she has somehow chosen the precisely wrong word: *We?* Why did she say 'we'?"

Mother Adeline hits it like a hawk on a rabbit. "We? Her majesty does not deign to grant a boon to her poor subjects?"

"I don't think ..." The Doctor starts to say something but only says that.

"*We* do not wish to play." Mother Adeline laughs in a way that could turn milk. "I am the mother of a queen. Should I have said, 'I humbly beseech you to play, your Royal Majesty?' Should I bend the knee and grovel so that you might condescend to play for us, Miss Marcella Veronica? Would you have your mother beg?"

"Mother Adeline," Sunshine says.

Looking at his sister, Adam thinks, Sunshine's scared.

"For Chrissake," The Doctor says.

"For Christ's sake indeed," Mother Adeline says. She quotes a lethal favorite by Mary Baker Eddy: "'The entire education of children should be such as to form habits of obedience to the moral and spiritual law.'"

Sunshine gets to her feet. She looks miserable and confused. She looks like a cat in the rain. "I'm sorry. I just was drawing ... I didn't want to play. I just didn't want to ..."

Do not cry, Adam Nichols thinks. *Don't let her get you to crying that easy. You're probably going to cry, but make the bitch earn it.*

"Is that all, your Majesty?" says Mother Adeline. "Is that stammered foolishness your apology?"

The Doctor says, "The child did ..."

Mother Adeline gives him a look that is a warning and says worse than that because it says almost everything.

The Doctor says nothing.

Mother Adeline cites Mary Baker Eddy: "'A mother is the strongest educator.' I am about to educate Her Royal Highness."

Mother Adeline rises. "Come with me," she says. She takes Sunshine by the hand. She leads her down the hall. Sunshine walks without bending her knees.

—She beat her? The psychiatrist does not sound non-directive. He sounds judgmental.

—The world was more Calvin than Freud back then. Your parents hit you. It was what parents did.

—The Doctor had a razor strop. Mother Adeline's instructional instrument was the hairbrush.

Mother Adeline and Sunshine are back soon. "So, then," Mother Adeline says, "now, perhaps, Marcella Veronica will consent to play the Schumann."

Sunshine stands in the center of the parlor and looks like she has eaten something that had a too strong smell and too sharp taste. Her face is very white and her eyes are hard and shining.

What a good kid, Adam Nichols thinks. *What a real good kid she is.*

Because Sunshine says, "I would prefer not to."

"Marcella Veronica," Mother Adeline says, "think about what it is that you are saying."

"No," Sunshine says, "I would prefer not to."

I'll bet she could spit right now if she had to. Sunshine is just swell is what she is, Adam thinks.

"Very well," Mother Adeline says.

Adam Nichols looks to The Doctor. The Doctor's eyes are lowered. He doesn't say anything.

"Mary Baker Eddy teaches 'Children should obey their parents; insubordination is an evil.'"

The Doctor doesn't say anything.

"Come with me," Mother Adeline says.

This time, Sunshine and Mother Adeline are gone for quite a while and there is a good deal of noise: the sounds of hitting and the sounds a child makes when she's being hit.

The Doctor turns the pages of the *Sporting News*. Aloud, he reads, "Despite the shady nature of the mat game as it is practiced today, no one who loves the ancient sport dare cast any aspersions upon the quintessentially American athlete Frank Gotch. When he tossed his robe to his trainer-manager Jim Asbel, Gotch said, 'Keep this to remember me by,' though doubtless the faithful Asbel, who had seen Gotch in battles glorious against George Hackenschmidt, The Russian Lion ..."

"Don't you think ..." Adam Nichols says, just as a door

squeaks open down the hall.

Mother Adeline and Sunshine return to the parlor. Sunshine's face is red and wet.

"Would you like to play Schumann's 'Scenes from Childhood' now?" says Mother Adeline.

"Goddamnit," The Doctor says, quiet.

"Yes, I would," Sunshine says.

"I thought you might."

"But I can't," Sunshine says, as she raises her hands and then takes the little finger of the left between her right thumb and forefinger, "because I'm afraid I've broken my finger." And she quickly bends her little finger back until there is bone snap muffled by flesh as the blood drains out of her face and she crumples down to the floor in a faint, smiling.

VII

NOW I LAY ME

Adam Nichols could not sleep that night. Usually, he felt tired and good at night up in Michigan and fell asleep quick and slept sound but tonight he felt heavy but not tired and did not feel good. So as he lay awake, he thought about the many places he had fished in his life and he thought about the many places he would fish and he thought about a big, two-hearted river but then he thought he saw himself wading in the water and all around him were dead trout, furry with white fungus, slapping uncaring against a rock in the meaningless way of death, floating belly up in the little pools and shadows beneath the trees and that made him sick.

Adam decided to stop thinking about fishing. He was just cold awake and he started praying. *Now I lay me ...* He prayed for all the people he had ever known, although he was not exactly sure what it was he prayed for those people. He probably asked for God's blessing for each of them, although he was not sure what a blessing was or how it might be deemed granted. He prayed for Jesus to take them all to heaven, which is what he thought he was supposed to do, although he imagined heaven to be little more than a clean, well-lighted place and was not in the least certain why anyone would want to go there. *Now I lay me ...* He mostly prayed because remembering the names of all the people he had ever known took up a lot of time and if you cannot sleep then you need something to take up the time. And if you cannot take up all the time with the names of all the people you have ever known, then you can try to remember the names of all the animals you have seen at the zoo, or you can remember all the names of birds from *Youth's Guide to Birds of the World*: canary and parakeet and stone curlew and quail and little ringed plover and oystercatcher and that's a funny name but what it does is catch oysters and the night is so heavy and you are never more alone than you are at night *Now I lay me* poor bird poor mourning dove poor whippoorwill poor Sunshine with her broken finger and two spankings in a single day *Now I lay me* and God granteth a blessing upon Sunshine and *Now I lay me* counting in the dark the sun gone down but the sun also rises and God bless The Doctor the poor Doctor and ...

He heard them.

He heard The Doctor and Mother Adeline. He heard their voices but not what they were saying.

He heard them moving quietly in the cottage.

Adam Nichols got up quietly. He had on his long underwear. He slipped his feet into leather slippers. He tried to walk in the totally silent, pigeon-toed way the Indians walked.

He followed Mother Adeline and The Doctor outside. He did not let them see him. There was a full moon. Mother Adeline and The Doctor were not talking now. The Doctor had grandfather's .32 caliber pistol. He held it casually at his side as he and Mother Adeline walked down to the little pier.

—This was a dream you had as a child? the psychiatrist said.
—No. You're a fool. You understand nothing. It was no dream. This is what happened.

1961
Mayo Clinic
Rochester, Minnesota

There is an old man on a gurney and his belly is big and his legs are splayed and scrawny and a tired line of drool runs down at the left side of his slack mouth. You might think he looks like an old lion who could no longer hide from the hunters and has taken a bad shot but has not yet earned the *coup de grâce*, but the old man would not say that if you asked him and he were able to respond.

He would say he looks like a tired old man.

They have just shot lightning through his head. It is like an electrical explosion in his brain. They have tried to blast away whatever has made him sad but something else has happened because he is no longer here not here and he is *Now I lay me* looking down at himself without pity nor irony and *pues y nada* and now he goes drifting off drifting away

I'm lighting out.

VII

THE STRANGE COUNTRY

—*Hey-aye-hey!*
—Gilby Edwards. It is you.
—Goddamn right, kid. Who else? Teddy Roosevelt? Buffalo Bill Bullshit?
—You're dead, Gilby.
—Goddamn right.
—You're a ghost.
—Yeah. Hell, yes. Old Gilby gone Jiibay and that's a fact. No bullshit.
—And kid, now you free like First Ojibway boy. You travel in spirit and in the world of the spirits.
—Look down. See everyone. See everything.

The moonlight made everything clear and black and white. Mother Adeline and The Doctor were in the boat. The Doctor was no longer rowing. The boat rocked gently and the water lapped softly against it. The pistol lay by The Doctor on the seat.

The Doctor said—and Adam Nichols heard him plainly—"This is what the Ojibway say. Tribe have bitch woman, man have bitch wife, *hey-aye-hey*, take bitch in canoe and send her to Neebanaw and Winona!"

"You are drunk," Mother Adeline said. "Mrs. Eddy writes, 'The drunkard thinks he enjoys drunkenness, and you cannot make the inebriate leave his besottedness, until his physical sense of pleasure yields to a higher sense.' You have no higher sense. You are a heathen and a savage. You have chosen to be despicable."

"Injun smart. Plenty ghosts in lake. Damn right." The Doctor laughed.

"The Church of Christ Scientist teaches us about ghosts. '... ghosts are not realities, but traditional beliefs, erroneous and man-made ...' In short ... there are no such things."

You might think the ghosts in the lake had been listening. It was like they were actors who had been diligent at all their rehearsals and were now determined to give a superb performance. The Jiibay of Ghost Lake rippled up through the black water. They were shimmering and glowing white. They made a sound that was something like laughter but had no joy in it. It was a dead sound and pinched. The women-ghosts had black holes for eyes. They had black holes for mouths. They had no flesh. They were horrible and ghastly and did a fluttering dance on the water all around the boat.

"What is it you intend?" Mother Adeline asked The Doctor. She sounded calm. She seemed to take no notice of the ghosts that had risen from the lake.

"I mean to take your life," The Doctor said. The Doctor raised the .32 caliber Smith & Wesson.

The ghosts encircled the boat. Their fleshless arms were waving and they moved in a parody of a dance. They sang a song that had no breath in it, no life.

Then the ghosts were a shimmering dome of dead white light that fell upon the boat and covered it.

Adam Nichols could see nothing.

But before he left the world of the spirits he heard the shot. It was sharp and had the flickering echo you hear when a bullet is fired over a body of water.

It sounded like a killing shot.

46

1935
Ghost Lake, Michigan

Each time Toby snapped off a shot with the .22 caliber Winchester, a black squirrel fell. He shot six squirrels with six bullets. It made for a good day. Toby's being a good shot surprised Adam Nichols because the boy's mother had not been a good shot, not anything like it, though she had tried to learn several times to please him. She tried to do a number of things to please him and never did until at last she despaired of pleasing him and he grew weary of her attempts.

Toby pleased him a good deal. Toby seemed to do it without trying. Adam Nichols thought he would have liked Toby even if Toby were not his son.

In the early afternoon, they set up camp by the shore of Ghost Lake. They were hungry. Adam Nichols showed his son how to dress the squirrels, how to slip the furry skin down their legs as though you were removing little pants. Toby laughed at that.

In addition to all the squirrel, Adam Nichols cooked up a can of pork and beans and a can of spaghetti. It was not real camping food, but the kind of camping food he had eaten when he was a very young boy. And besides, Adam Nichols told Toby, "If we were willing to carry it, we have every right to eat it."

Toby laughed. "I don't think I've ever been hungrier," Toby said.

It came to Adam Nichols that he liked this boy quite a lot. He loved this boy.

And as he watched the boy eating, he wondered if the boy liked him or loved him.

Isn't that a question? The Doctor's ghost said that. *Isn't that a question you ask your whole life.* Adam Nichols was not surprised that the ghost was here. If ghosts had a sense of smell, The Doctor always liked cooking over a campfire and had taught Adam. Though he saw nothing like it, Adam could easily imagine The Doctor's ghost as a wavering image just over the rising hot air of the fire.

Adam Nichols did not think Toby heard or saw anything. He could understand that. The Doctor was Toby's grandfather but The Doctor's ghost belonged only to Adam Nichols.

Adam Nichols had a good day with Toby.

That is why fathers have sons, The Doctor's ghost told him.

—And you believe this? the psychiatrist asked. He
could not make himself seem non-directive. He
sounded amazed. He did not sound Catholic.
—Yes, I believe.
—You believe your father's ghost was there and
talking to you?
—I believe in my father's ghost who art or art not in
heaven, depending on whether or not our Holy
Mother Church teaches the truth about suicides,
which The Doctor may or may not have been. I
believe in the ghost of Gilby Edwards, who might
well be drunk and whooping and dancing in the
Happy Hunting Ground. I believe in the ghosts in
Ghost Lake who are mean and bitchy and abideth
a'bitching forever and ever amen. I believe in the
ghost of the dead man I spoke to as I carried him to
the dressing station in the war to end all wars that
didn't end war not for shit, old son, not for shit. I
believe in the ghost of the bullfighter Tonio
Mendoza who twice had the horns pass through him
and died calling to the crowd *I guess I have showed I
can take it like a man!* I believe in the ghosts of
Michigan and Cuba and the ghosts of Paris by night
and the Serengeti by day and the glorious ghosts of
the Abraham Lincoln Brigade ... *Viva la quince
brigada!*
—I believe in the ghosts of all the people I used to
be before becoming this broken down human ruin
with a rock-hard liver and bones that creak and a
hollow vacancy in the belfry and nothing but
memory which even now fades away like morning
dew. I believe in the ghosts of wineskins and the
ghosts of making love in the afternoon and of
running with the bulls and of laughing and fishing
for marlin and of drinking beer and the howitzers'
great boom, the ghosts, all dead and gone, dead and
gone, all ghosts.
—And if there are no ghosts, how is it that we carry

them with us wherever we go?
I believe.
Help my unbelief, give me strength, I believe I
believe.
—Let us pray.
—Now I lay me *y pues y nada* and I pray to ghosts
my ghost to keep and welcome my ghost to the land
of ghosts *y pues y nada y pues y nada* for *pues* is the
kingdom and the power of ghosts forever and ghost
amen my ghosts amen
amen amen.

Across the open mouth of the tent, Adam Nichols had fixed
cheesecloth so there would be no mosquitoes and Toby was
asleep in the tent. He slept the way boys sleep when they have
had a very good day.

But Adam Nichols could not sleep. So he had a drink of
whiskey from a silver flask. Then he had another. There was a
three-quarter moon, but still he started a fire with chips of pine
and he sat by it and looked out at Ghost Lake and saw a mist.

Then The Doctor's ghost was sitting beside him.

Adam Nichols did not have to look to know that but he turned
his head and there was The Doctor, a ghost.

I like it when you tell the boy about Africa.

"I will take him there someday," Adam Nichols said. "I will. He
will like Africa. He will not be afraid. I will teach him not to be
afraid."

I am sorry I never went to Africa, The Doctor said. I am sorry I
never took you to Africa.

"You taught me to hunt and fish," Adam Nichols said. "You
taught me what I had to do so I could begin to know Africa."

Adam Nichols smiled. He held out the silver flask of whiskey to
his father's ghost. "Would you like a drink?"

I would, the ghost said, but did not move, so Adam took a
drink.

Then, "There is that which I wish to ask you," he said,
formally.

You may, the ghost of his father formally answered.

"I need to know the truth," Adam Nichols said.

There is a truth that comes at first light that is no longer true by noon, the ghost said. That is a saying in Africa.

"The Maasai, it is one of their sayings," Adam Nichols said. "Yes. But might you then tell me what happened that night?"

Adam Nichols and the ghost of The Doctor, his father, Chadbourne Nichols, MD, were both talking about the night on the lake when Mother Adeline and the Doctor were in the boat surrounded by all the ghosts and then the ghosts fell upon them and the gun was fired.

The ghost explained, What happened that night was, she killed me.

IX

THE END OF SOMETHING

July 2, 1961
Ketchum, Idaho

It was early and he was the only one up. It was a beautiful morning. There were no clouds. There was sunshine.

Then he remembered that Gary Cooper was dead. Cooper had been dead for—was it a month?

Cooper, yes, Coop had beat him to the barn. Cooper him gone Jiibay.

He went to the gun cabinet. He opened it. There was only one pistol inside. It was an old .32 caliber Smith & Wesson, manufactured in Springfield, Massachusetts. It was his grandfather's gun. It was then his father's gun. His grandfather and his father had both used it.

When he was thirty, Mother Adeline sent him the gun for his birthday, along with a note:

> *My Dear Son,*
> *I thought you might want this or have sentimental feelings for it. Though yours is not always a practical nature, I trust you will find some use for it.*

The note was signed: *With a Mother's Eternal Love.*

He did not take the pistol from the cabinet. He took the Boss shotgun he had bought at Abercrombie and Fitch.

He went into the front foyer. He liked the way the light struck the oak-paneled walls and the floor. It was like being in a museum or in a church. It was a well-lighted place and it felt clean and airy.

He whispered a prayer.

Carefully, he lowered the butt of Boss shotgun to the floor. He leaned forward. The twin barrels were cold circles in the scarred tissue just above his eyebrows.

He tripped both triggers.

GUIDANCE

7:15 A.M. – Before First Period
Guidance Department

They are all here, all morning coffee and long silences and shrugs and sighs and nerves: Dr. Lytell, the district psychologist, Stacy Navores, principal, Andrea Evans, head of guidance, the counselors, two new hires, so new they probably have yet to frame their diplomas, Bob Biondi, expert at finding college funds, Macy Gaston, knows how to get a wacky kid classified and into an alternative school and one-two-three *out! of! here!* and, of course, the veteran, Theo DeWalt, age sixty-five, not so long in the tooth but definitely light in the hair, a shiny head framed in fringe that would make Rogaine toss up its hands in defeat.

Of course, it is DeWalt the kids will want to see.

Because this is a heavy one. It's sad, it's just so goddamned sad is what it is. High school is not all quadratic equations and SAT scores and band trip and prom and career paths to tomorrow and smoking in the boys' room and cutting fifth period; there is *sadness*, sadness beyond the loss of the homecoming game or the leukemia diagnosis for that favorite German teacher or that mangled bloody stupidity of alcohol and kids and a train crossing.

This one is the saddest sad: A student suicide.

7:30 A.M. – Main Hallway

The busses unloaded in the circle drive at the main entrance to Hillman-Forest Lake High School. A ghost entered with the students that sunny Monday, first day back after Spring break. Being a ghost was quite new and sometimes confusing, although not in a bad way, for Kelli Wrightmann. When she had been alive and thought about the *transitioning* from life to death, when she had resolved to kill herself, she had considered "ghostliness" a possibility. *Who really knew, right?* As a ghost, she'd rather expected to feel, well, sort of damp, maybe like a mildewing army blanket, and perhaps awkward and sluggish, as though slogging through a rain-soaked cemetery, but what she mostly felt was the welcome absence of that damn backpack that never settled right; it always rubbed low on her left shoulder blade.

It did not surprise her that she was paid no notice by students zigging and zagging as though they had to get somewhere that mattered, or by teachers, lolling at classroom doors, supposedly monitoring the halls, or slipping into a faculty restroom for that quick pee stop before classes, or by the youngish guard with the overdone haircut at the security desk at West and North Hall, who used to look at her <u>tush</u> more than might have been necessary to keep it secure.

Invisibility. It was like having a super-power or something, Kick-Ass Hit Girl! Huntress! Invisible Woman! All you do is die and benefits begin immediately!

Her parents had not been able to see her, hear her (or for that matter touch or feel or probably taste her). She'd checked it out. After she'd come back, must have been about two days or so after she died (no clue as to why you had a waiting period!), she'd hovered awhile in the living room just above the 52" Bravia (volume set at a "mutter level," sincere Rachel Maddow sincerely upset about something sincerely upsetting), and Mom and Dad were on the sofa, a cushion separating them, wineglasses in hands uniting them.

They looked old, they looked saggy, they looked bad.

And Kelli said, speaking in a way that felt no less real than when she'd been alive, "Hello, and I just want to tell you, you have no reason to blame yourselves ..."

She could hear herself. They could not hear her.

Mom said, "I don't understand. I do not. I don't understand." Her voice sounded flattened out and stretched and Kelli detected a not so teeny-tiny jolt of Valium working alongside the wine.

Dad said, "I don't know how she could have ..."

Get pills. Easy to do in any high school in U S of A. Put pills in mouth. Swallow, swallow, swallow, with a Dr. Pepper. All gone and now I lay me, and then I am all gone ...

"... because it is so *wrong*. She was a wonderful girl, but it was the wrongest thing she could have done. Wrongest thing she ever did."

Uh-uh, not *wrong. No way.*

It felt like she yelled it, but neither the Mater nor the Pater heard.

So—an experiment?—she yanked Mom's hair and uh-uh, zero in the way of response, and she flip-snapped her index finger off the bulby tip of Dad's nose, and nothing.

Kelli Wrightmann, you are a hundred percent solid gone *ghost* is whatchoo be. "I don't understand," Mom said.

Redundantly

"... something we did ..."

... bogus psychology ... When I was little, you made me eat asparagus even though I hated the way it made my pee smell ... had to kiss Aunt Sonya, whose breath stunk like a javelina in heat

... Made me study and get good grades and sometimes made me stop studying and go out with my friends when you were worried about all the pressure I put on myself ...

"... didn't do ..."

... you did not let me get an iguana when I was in fourth grade; I'd have named it Fluffy ... Instead of going to Disneyworld, you thought you could satisfy me with 101 Dalmatians on Ice, and all those goddamn black spots skating around, I had vertigo for six months ...

"Oh, my God," Dad said.

And just beneath his wet eyes, he masked his face with his hand. Nobody ever sounded more bewildered when he said, "What did we do that was so wrong?"

You didn't. Kelli Wrightmann, ghost, did not mouth the words but she thought them and perhaps even wished Mom and Dad could hear her: *It's not your fault. There is no fault. This was my decision. I do not regret it.*

And Kelli Wrightmann, ghost, saw them grieving and crumpling, knew they would never, could never understand.

7:40 A.M. – Before First Period
The Halls

Not so strangely, the halls of Hillman-Forest Lake High School were more quiet than usual, but she caught flicks and snippets:

"Sad … I prayed for her when I heard …"

Thanks.

"I hope she's with Jesus …"

Maybe you didn't pray hard enough … Oh, let me check … Nope, no Jesus. Then … I'm sorry. I know you mean well. You can believe what you want to, okay? For me, not right now, anyway, there's no Jesus in the scenario. Maybe it's different for others …

"Maybe she thought she'd come back as a zombie, huh?"

"You're not funny. You're an asshole."

Agreed. Not funny. Asshole. I'm gonna haunt you. Boo!

Yeah, Let's go Ghost Hunters (Ghost Hunter Academy? Ghost Hunters International? Ghost Hunters Glee Edition?*): Today's episode: High School Ghost Haunts Asshole!*

"… didn't seem depressed …"

Wasn't. Am not.

"… Facebook, just fine …"

"… in chorus. Sang pretty … Not *American Idol* or anything …"

Not American Idol. Not Norah Jones. Not Robyn. Not Bristol Palin. Not Katie Couric or Hillary Clinton or Lindsay (loop d loop) Lohan or Fat Ass Kardashian. Not the Queen of the May, June, or July, or Miss Pancakes at the State Fair, or Putnam County Spelling Bee Champion. Just a pretty good kid, is what I am—was—that's what I was, was I, sez me.

That's about it …

8:40 A.M. – End of Home Room Period

PA announcement: … students and staff remember and pray for … a junior, Key Club member … student ambassador … need to talk … counselors will be available throughout the day … pass from your teacher or …

1:00 P.M.
Guidance Department

Mr. DeWalt had the biggest office in the department, meaning there was room enough for him, a desk and file cabinet, and two other people—as long as all three weren't breathing either in or out simultaneously. Theo DeWalt had begun his career as an English teacher, but switched to guidance early on. Long ago he'd been married, and then got divorced and stayed that way. He could have taken an ultra-sweet early retirement package at fifty-five but said "Uh-uh" because, as he said (and said and said—with your AARP card comes a tendency to repeat yourself): "I love the kids." And you didn't mind when DeWalt said it, because he said it without irony or Ned Flanders cornball "holier than thou" zeal.

The school psychologist, Marty Lytell, ordinarily a youthful forty, today, as old a forty as you can be and still be forty, sat across the desk, not looking at DeWalt, weary-bleary eyes slowly scanning years of kids' pictures on the wall: *Kids from the 1970s to the now. Fading Kodachrome to Epson ink jet ...* Smiling kids.

"I hate it the worst," Lytell said. "Give me stanines and percentiles. That's easy stuff. Or I check a student's ACT and GPA and tell him if he ought to go to Monmouth or the Marines. Even get your doctor to back off the Ritalin if you're gone zombie or get a DCFS rescue squad to save you from your diddling step-daddy ..." He sighed. "I can do all that.

"But something like this, shit. None of us even had a clue."

DeWalt said nothing.

"There are *supposed* to be warning signs: Disinterest in favorite school and extracurricular activities. Withdrawing from family and friends or friends. A goddamned checklist for school shrinkologists, but there was none of that ... You saw her just last week, right? How was she then?"

"She seemed fine," DeWalt said.

You could almost hear Lytell thinking, *It makes no sense, it makes no sense ...* He said, "She was a good kid."

"Yes."

"And now I don't know what to say to a kid who asks why her friend killed herself."

"Maybe you don't say anything." DeWalt spoke quietly. "Maybe you listen."

Lytell shook his head. "The non-directive bullshit, nah. They want to hear something. They're kids. They *need* to hear something. And I just don't know what to tell 'em." DeWalt's face was blank: a non-directive face. "I can't tell you," DeWalt said.

"So we do the best we can," Lytell said, rising.

"That's what everybody does," Mr. DeWalt said.

3:45 P.M. – After School
Guidance Department

Everyone in Guidance had gone home except Theo DeWalt. He seemed to be waiting, not impatiently, exactly, but definitely with expectation. He was sitting at his desk when the ghost of Kelli Wrightmann entered.

"Mr. DeWalt?" she said.

"He said, "It's good to see you, Kelli."

And she felt a flutter, not like a tic of the heart, because there was no longer that sort of corporeality to her being, but a wavering of herself.

"You can see me, Mr. DeWalt. You can hear me."

He nodded.

The understanding came in a spiking instant that was not reason but intuition.

Ghosts do not haunt places.

Ghosts haunt people.

Ghosts haunt the people who are responsible for their being ghosts.

Ghosts haunt the people who are responsible for their deaths.

"My mother and father are very sad," Kelli said.

"Yes."

"My aunts and uncles and cousins, the family, and my friends and my teachers, I think they are all very sad."

"Yes, I think so," Mr. DeWalt said.

"You're not sad."

No, he told her, he was not.

She told him she thought she understood, truly, but she wanted him to tell her once more, to tell her again.

He did.

... and sometimes, sometimes you find a terrific kid, a wunderkind, not the child prodigy in math or violin playing or

tennis, just a perfect kid, a golden child who hints at what the race might become with another evolutionary jump and God's acquiescence. Perfect Boy is seventeen years old, nary a pimple nor bleb nor blemish, nothing of the awkward, the gangly, the ungainly, no awkward stage, not like other boys, all elbows and Oops, with noses they might someday grow into and flap-a-dap ears, this one all hunched over because he feels too short to be so tall, this one hanging a mumbling head because his chin is too weak, this one gawking at his super-sized feet and struggling to find an answer to your "Hello."

Perfect Boy—a kid like Adam, there on the wall, that's his picture from 1978—a kid called Jim or Dave or Bob or Eric or Ron (never a Marv[in] or Kirk[land] or Connor? Connie? Connie? Get serious! or Jeff(ery) or Max(well)(millian)(imus), a beautifully All-American homegrown boy, who cheers a Payton Manning pass, who grins at a fresh-waxed 1968 vintage Mustang, who revels in the fresh baked smell from a bakery, who just flat-out smiles at a sunny day ...

This perfect-in-his-youth human being is, right now, just as right as right can be, and will never be more right.

And certainly we have every great once in a while the Perfect Girl, a bipedalled splendor, a stunning singularity. Perfect Girl, you need do nothing with your hair but shake your exquisite head, your teeth are amped for the high wattage smile, and old men grow wistful and melancholy when they hear your laugh, your pure and spontaneous dancing joy sounds. You run so fast with never a hesitation, trip, stumble or fall and every note you sing is in tune and your very presence will seem to gather all the air in a room about you as you enter.

Wunderkinder. Faultless and Perfected, these young ones selected by Cosmic Lottery or DNA or Who Knows? seem ordained for a life of great gifts and many blessings.

But not so, not so.

Because it is only NOW, in this ah, too brief span of years we call youth that they are the Golden Ones, so very like unto Gods.

And some of them—not all, but a few, the hyper-perceptive amongst these discerning, sensitive, intelligent, good young people—have a sense of what will come in the years ahead.

They fear that, Shakespeare notwithstanding, age will stale and custom wither ... They are now at the pinnacle, but from this *point on, whether the gradual descent down that the clichéd slippery slope or a sudden freefall into the abyss, it's going to be down, down, down, down!*

Perhaps down into that life of quiet desperation, a half-life, if you will, of dreams gone to dust and abandoned, but still painful because they cannot be forgotten, of achievements that feel as though they've achieved nothing, of frustrations and disappointments. There comes a time of no disenchantment— because there is no longer any enchantment.

And if you are of a theatrical bent, you identify too, too well with both Willie and Biff of Death of a Salesman.

And every minor catastrophe, three steps backward for every half-step ahead, every time Xanax / Coke / Cutty Sark / a straitjacket would help, every loss anticipated or "who saw that one coming" is marked upon the calendar of your body with dimming eyesight, and abundance of drool for the pillow, and sagging buttocks, and bunions and fingernail fungus and skin going to crêpe ...

And if you have the intimation when you are sixteen, or seventeen or eighteen or perhaps—perhaps even a few years more!—if you come to understand "This is as good as it gets!" then you also comprehend choices made by James Dean and Jimi Hendrix and Kurt Cobain and Marilyn Monroe ...

And if you are of a literary bent, you think about that athlete dying young in Mr. A.E. Housman's poem, and, well, not such a bad deal, okay, because the alternative will most likely be mediocrity or, let's stay literary here, "a tale full of sound and fury told by an idiot signifying nothing"—except far more boring.

Life is a choice.

You are not obliged to choose it.

But no one seems to understand.

No one but Mr. Theo DeWalt.

Mr. Theo DeWalt, who loves kids, and understands and helps you understand and, when the time is right, offers his approval.

This is what Theo DeWalt again tells Kelli Wrightmann, now a ghost, on this sunny Monday afternoon.

Then there are other ghosts with them. Theo DeWalt has been a guidance counselor for many years and the office would be quite crowded if ghosts were not so immaterial.

To Mr. Theo DeWalt, Kelli Wrightmann says, "Thank you."

Mr. DeWalt's loving gaze takes in all those who have come to him.

He says, "You are welcome."

ROBOT

I am eighty-one years old so I have decided to become a robot. It is really quite affordable now. When I tell Sondra, she says, "*Oy, Shlemiel Schlimazl.*" She laughs. Sondra is also eighty-one, we share a birthday, and her laugh has mostly not changed over time, a little more dry perhaps, with a hint of wispiness, but it is still quite the good laugh.

"I am serious," I say.

"All right, you are a serious *Shlemiel Schlimazl.*" Sondra has called me *Shlemiel Schlimazl* since perhaps the second or third year of our marriage; it followed a time when I was drinking too much and she was contemplating an affair with the pretentious owner of an art gallery. I stopped drinking and she stopped contemplating and we started to have a great deal more fun with one another. *Shlemiel Schlimazl* is redundantly messed-up Yiddish. A *Shlemiel*, you see, *is* a *Schlimazl*, and vice-versa, although one supposedly implies a tad more klutziness than the other, although no one is quite sure which is the klutzy one.

Sondra laughs. "A robot ..."

Some twenty-two years back, the cancer and that first surgery, I remember sitting in the waiting room and wondering if ever again I'd hear Sondra laugh. I did not tear up or anything like that—I am not a sentimental man and, as Sondra would tell you, she is not sentimental, either—but I think that was the very first time I realized I could lose her.

The surgery was textbook successful, the surgeon self-congratulatory in that way surgeons have. All would be well. Sondra did not even require chemo. Very little pain afterward. A visiting nurse each day for a week. Understanding plastic surgeons for reconstructions and diligent internists and thoughtful nursing personnel. It was a decent enough bout of cancer as such things go.

"Sometimes lucky," Sondra summed it up. She quoted a Yiddish proverb. "Better an ounce of luck than a pound of gold."

By the way, I suppose I should tell you I am not Jewish—nor Christian, nor Muslim, nor much of anything. Midwestern, perhaps. Sondra was raised vaguely Jewish, like many of her era, a rich cultural heritage—chopped liver, matzo balls, and Henny Youngman—and a theology solidly based on, eh, who knows, not entirely impossible that there could maybe be a God.

You could say, though, we both believe in proverbs, and the Yiddish ones, as pessimistic as the Spanish, usually are the most humorous.

"Oh, I am not going full robot all at once," I explain. "It makes more sense to move into it slowly." It is all so simple nowadays: outpatient surgery / robotics.

"Silly, silly ... *Du bist er Shlemiel Schlimazl.*"

It is because of the guitar that I have decided to start with my hands. You see, once upon a time, so far back in the day that it might have been the morning of the day, a time when there were still such analog and wonderful items as phonograph records, there were guitar players like the three Kings: BB, Albert, and Freddie. They played quite different styles, uniquely their own, but they all understood that the right note in the right place at the right time was all you needed and that was how I tried to play, and, for some years there, had some success, but then, after a time in which it seemed there were no guitar players and only supposed musical instruments—SYNTHESIZERS as in synthetics!—there came the Dominance of the Shredders, most of them with hair that looked as though it had exploded out of their brains, and they could zip about ten gazillion notes at you like steroidal swarms of bees and if there was not one right note in the onslaught, how could you even notice.

I gave up the guitar about then. And to make certain I had truly given it up, I became a CPA—and no one is more "Former Guitar Player" than a CPA.

Throughout our marriage, Sondra has often said, "Why don't you take up guitar again?"

Sometimes I would say, "There is something offensive about a guitar playing CPA."

"You could play for me."

"What if you did not like what I played? Or the way I played?"

"You *are* a *Shlemiel Schlimazl.*"

But I am now eighty-one. I have stripped off my CPAness. I am retired. I have Medicare and Medicare Super-Plus! (thank you Bernie Sanders), so I will get some robot hands with robot fingers that will move like no blood filled meat and sinew ever could and I will open up full automatic rat-a-tat-tat every time and I will mow 'em down, I will mow you down!

That's what I tell Sondra about my robot fingers.

"Now you are definitely talking sense," Sondra says.

"Now you are talking irony."

"Irony is irony. And sarcasm is sarcasm."

I do not tell Sondra that robot fingers on a guitar will not feel anything, not a thing.

<hr>

"And then what?" Sondra wants to know.

"Nothing ostentatious"

"Hmm?"

"Knees. The senior citizen blue-plate special. Knees and hips."

It might be the Yoga class that is guiding the decision. One of those New Age things you do to pretend you are not heading into old age.

Stress relief. I needed it. It was about fourteen years ago. I did not want to start drinking and Sondra's cancer was back with an *Ah Ha, GOTCHA!* This time, the Three Musketeers of Misery: Radiation and Chemo and Surgery.

Let us say, Sondra did not laugh much for a time. Most in her situation do not.

Oh, perhaps some do. *Hey, you thought that was vomiting? Check this out! Hey, is the light reflecting off my bald head bothering you ...*

And so I signed up for a church basement Yoga class. We had perhaps eighteen to twenty New Age novices ranging from Emerging Adolescent to Full Geezer. We attempted the Downward Facing Dog, the Half Frog Pose, the Feathered Peacock

Pose, the Dead Duck on Table with Its Legs Stuck Up, etc.

It was not for me. Bend and stretch and hurt, lose balance, fall on elbow, etc. But I discovered that some degree of anxiety was alleviated when I went for a walk, a long walk of three to four miles. You can concentrate on one foot in front of the other and that is the sole focal point, simple and relieving. (Charles Dickens is reputed to have done twelve to fifteen miles every day of his adult life. He died at age fifty-eight.)

Listen to your body. That was a mantra Yoga instructor drilled into us. *Listen to your body,* drilled she, *"listen to your body."*

Feeling like Sisyphus on level ground on those hikes, but somehow less bad and more okay, I heard my body speaking to me.

My hips and knees said, "Replace me."

My ass said, "I'm dragging."

When I was a kid, there was a TV show called *The Six Million Dollar Man.* After being severely injured, an astronaut, Steve Austin, gets bionic prosthetics: an arm, both legs, and a left eye. Steve Austin was portrayed by an alleged actor named Lee Majors, whose face had all the expressiveness of aluminum siding.

You can be sure, however, that among my hormonal high school crowd (male), there was considerable pondering concerning the likelihood of Steve's having had another bionic add-on, one that could not even be alluded to on Prime Time Network Television in those innocent years: He had a uniquely male enhancement. (Get it, nudge, nudge?)

And how might he ...

Oh, my god, god, God, GOD! It's huge and it glows and it spins and it vibrates and it's warm and it hums the "Battle Hymn of the Republic." Giveittome gimmee ... Oh! Ooh! O O O O!!!!

When I was a child, I spake as a child and grew hoot-owl horny as a child, but now that I am an old fart ...

I mean, if you watch any cable, you know my demographic is Cialis, Viagra, implant, super-pump, testosterone, natural and unnatural supplement, etc. Along with the Rascal scooter (Now you can have the mobility of an NHL goalie as long as your battery is charged) and the tripod cane (You won't fall on your stupid face unless you're so damned fat as well as unbalanced that you break the cane ...).

But no, I am not going to get my unit replaced. My libidinal urges for a while have hardly been urgent. Sex is mostly a memory and a nice warm feeling—a remembered feeling.

So I will keep my original John Thomas, limp though it has mostly been for quite a while now.

Confession: With a quite understandable fear of STDs, in my youth I nonetheless sowed my wild oats. Carefully. Three times.

But with Sondra, well, she is the only woman with whom I have had relations since she came into my life and certainly throughout our marriage I have been boringly faithful.

To state it as it is: Sondra was and is the only woman with whom I have wanted that sort of intimacy.

The past thirteen months, Sondra has not been interested in sex.

She has been too ill.

Trachst du auf di gis geyn tsu pishn? Sondra says. Yiddish proverb. Translation: Are you contemplating where the geese go to pee?

All right, proverbs. I reply, *Az mir pisht in shnay, vert a loch.* When you pee in the snow, it makes a hole.

Next stage in my robotic transition: A heart.

"*Oy,*" Sondra says, "Last year, you had a stress test. You had an ultrasound. You have the blood pressure of an Olympic boxer. Your heart is fine. Why would you want to replace it?"

I don't answer.

"*Shlemiel Schlimazl.*"

I do not tell her my heart is breaking. I do not tell my heart will break.

The final step: I will have my robot brain.

It will start out blank, of course, *tabula rasa*, un-apped iPad. But then they can transfer over my cognitive abilities. Ours was perhaps the last generation to learn the multiplication tables and I do not want to jettison that. I want to still be able to dazzle with "nine times nine is eighty-one."

I can have an improvement in memory, so that the tip-of-the-tongue song title no longer eludes me:

"Who Threw the Overalls in Mrs. Murphy's Chowder?"

"Stella by Starlight"

"Our Love is Here to Stay"

"It Had to Be You"

I think I want to remember the song titles and, for that matter, I want to remember the lyrics.

I am speaking of songs like

"Sweet and Lovely"

"You Were Meant for Me"

I am speaking of a song like

"What'll I Do?"

I will keep all the memories, all the memories, and to be quite honest, those memories are primarily

Sondra & I

I & Sondra

The two of us as one ... Forgive the clichés, but isn't that what marriage is *supposed* to be?

And, even with the bumps and problems and fate and failures, we had—we *have* a marriage—we are

Sondra&I I&Sondra

We are—we are ...

Sondra is dying.

The return of the cancer.

The third time is the charm.

Inoperable. Untreatable. It's everywhere within her.

The painkillers are quite good. She does not hurt a great deal. Doctor Oncology predicts she has another six months.

So what I will do, when I have my robot brain installed, is ask them to leave out the cells and sensors and synapses of affect that permit or force one to feel, to have emotions. I will be intellectually aware, of course, I will know loss but I will not *feel* loss.

Because I could not continue, I could not.
Nor would I want to.
"My robot ..." Sondra reaches for me.
We hold hands.
Sondra asks, "Are you crying, my robot?"
"I am not yet a robot."
"No," Sondra says.
"You are my *Shlemiel Schlimazl.*"

THE STORY OF ALBERT GLUCKLICH
OR
WHAT THEY HAD IN COMMON

In the unpleasantness among the nations of the world that came about in 1914 was a private named Albert Glucklich who served in the army of the Kaiser. It happened that one moonless night an artillery bombardment began that was quite the splendid surprise, despite the best efforts of those at their listening posts in the saps and even an observation balloon which earlier had risen into the late afternoon sky to cheery *halloos* from both sides. The trenches of the opposing armies were no more than 200 meters apart and it was in this "No Man's Land," as it was poetically if not precisely called, that our private Albert Glucklich found himself part of an expeditionary squad advancing in the mud on their stomachs when the heavy guns commenced their work.

There were exploding noises and exploding lights and Albert wondered about the nature of the shelling: Might this be a "Box Barrage" or was it more rightly a "Search Barrage?" He wished he could ask his sergeant, who had two years of successful trench experience, having thus far not been killed nor seriously wounded, but his sergeant was not to be found nor were any of the others in the patrol because in the initial bursts Albert had been separated from them when he was blown up and out of his boots and his helmet disappeared and his two grenades and Mauser GEW 98 rifle were gone and now it came to him that he was alone and lying spread-eagled and not fully sensible in No Man's Land, and that despite his youth and dedication to the Fatherland, it was now plainly conceivable that he might die, notwithstanding the brass assurance of his "*Gott Mit Uns*" belt buckle; all in all, his prospects did not give him cause for optimism.

So Albert rose and ran in a sort of skittering, free-floating hazy manner more properly attributed to panic than purpose until he tripped upon something most ambiguous and gelatinous and he rose and tumbled headfirst down an incline of mud and then he lost his senses and then found them again and now he lay on uneven terrain, his head lower than his feet, in a broad and deep shell crater wherein he heard a surprised "*Qui est-il? Etes-vous un ami?*" from only a meter or so away.

Though as we all know the Kaiser did not prove victorious in the Great War, it was not because his troops lacked bayonets. The Kaiser's army developed and issued more types of bayonets than did all other combatant forces combined. Albert Glucklich no longer had his rifle nor his headgear nor his footwear, but he still possessed his saw tooth bayonet, which he yanked from its scabbard. Albert was terrified, and so it was terror that prompted his striking out with the bayonet, and perhaps terror, too, which prevented his following his training which had taught him to direct the bayonet at those vulnerable points of the enemy's body: the throat, left or right breast and left or right groin. Of course, it was dark, and our Albert might not have easily seen these priority targets, knowing only that "*Qui est-il? Etes-vous un ami?*" did not likely indicate he was in the company of a comrade.

The weapon found and pierced a breastbone, making removal of the blade highly problematic. When it entered the enemy's body, there was a muffled screech that traveled all the way up the arm of Albert Glucklich and into his own chest. It was similar to the sharp annoyance of hitting your crazybone. That startled Albert, quite badly, and so, with no true conscious thought, Albert tried to yank out his blade to strike again, the saw teeth caught and there was a sound not unlike that of a splintering soup bone and something thick and wet spurted on his hand and his enemy called out, loudly, but with much breathiness, "*S'il vous plaît arrêter! Vous m'avez tué. Je suis mort!*"

Just then a great shell burst overhead. In its light, Albert could see his bayonet and the man into whom he had thrust it. Though the man spoke French, he did not, Albert thought, look French. If he looked anything, he looked embarrassed and apologetic to be lying wounded and propped against the muddy crater wall. He looked like he regretted causing a bother with Albert Glucklich's bayonet protruding from of his chest.

"Do not ..." the man said. "Please."

"No," Albert answered.

Both men smiled at using English, but English at this time was rapidly becoming the universal language of commerce and warfare if not yet culture and, as it happened, Albert's English was considerably better than that of the average German soldier because not only had he studied at Gymnasium where he had learned such useful phrases as "This weather is not unpleasant in its season, no?" and "I am excited to be today attending the game of cricket" and "Please excuse me, stout woman, I did not intend to misstep upon your foot" but he had read *Pearson's* and *The Saturday Evening Post* magazines sent his mother before the war by a cousin in Chicago who worked as a cooper at the Schoenhofen Brewery.

"The others ..." the enemy said. There came a pause in the barrage and the light dwindled but Albert thought he could see his bayonet vibrate like a tuning fork. "I do not know. One moment we were all together and then the big guns started and they ran and I ran but not the same way that they did run ... I jumped in here to be safe."

"Hmm, I do guess that is what you thought." Albert Glucklich smiled, though he did not usually appreciate and seldom recognized irony. He had a bad metal taste on the back of his tongue and a fluttery feeling in his throat. "Maybe now you are safe," Albert said. "Maybe now you have found peace with this war."

"I do not know. If I shall know peace, it is not the sort of peace I wish to know, I do not think."

Albert said nothing.

"My name is Pascal Laurent," the man said.

Before he could think about it, Albert said, "I wish you had not told me that," but he was German and whether you are a swineherd crapping in the field alongside your pigs or Junker with dueling scar and the head of a wild boar over your mantel, there are rules of etiquette, one is obliged to be polite, and so he said, "I am Albert Glucklich."

They spoke for quite a while, in English and with occasional phrases in German and French. Sometimes they had to raise their voices as the long guns again began their pounding and rockets burst and there were times that it became difficult for Albert Glucklich to hear and times when it became difficult for Pascal Laurent to speak in what was becoming a rattling, wet wheeze.

Pascal Laurent and Albert Glucklich it seemed were both Roman Catholic. They both pretended not to remember when they had last been to confession because if they had admitted

remembering, then due to their sudden intimacy they might have had to say what they had confessed and neither wished to do that. In spite of his Gallic name, Pascal Laurent was pure Alsatian and like all Alsatians, who can happily spend Sunday afternoon in argument over recipes for *Choucroute Garnie*, he deemed himself a gourmet and, because he feared that soon food would no longer be of concern, he comforted himself by recalling all the good foods of his childhood: Christmas *Berauwecka* cakes and *kouglof*...

His mouth watering—for as we all know, Alsatian cuisine is Germanic to its soul and smallest potato—Albert felt obliged to speak of his own happy childhood memories. He wished he had cigarettes or a chew or a swallow of schnapps, they might have shared that, but he did not. He had nothing, not even boots. But a sharing of food and drink, yes, that would have been right considering the stories they were telling.

One story Pascal Laurent told was how when he went to war, his little cousin, Jean- Claude Martin, had given him the gift of a Hohner harmonica so that there could be "gay music in the trenches and spirits would not falter." There was a six-pointed star in a circle on the coverplate of the harmonica and Pascal and his friends often wondered if this meant the family of Matthias Hohner was Jewish. Pascal did not dislike the Jews, although his priest maintained they were not to be trusted. It was a very nice harmonica but the *Sergent-chef* did not care for any vulgar music and confiscated the Hohner to grind under his boot.

One story Albert Glucklich told was how when he was twelve, his Uncle Franz, who was a great traveler and a full member of the National Geographic Society, took him on holiday to ski at Schruns. The air was so cold and good you could bite it. Finding your footing, flying down the slope, your balance perfect as a gyro, you were no longer a man but a superman.

Then Albert and Pascal seemed to silently agree they could no longer speak of childhood because were they not now men?

Pascal Laurent asked his friend, "Albert, have you ever been with a woman?"

The sad truth, so sad that it made him want to weep, was No, Albert Glucklich had never been with a woman.

Pascal Laurent had been with women (Am I not French?) and now he had a woman, a woman to whom he was married these past eleven months, though he had been with her only the first month before the war effort demanded his presence in battle glorious. The woman of Pascal Laurent was named Arleta, and her father owned a bicycle shop in the old village of Riquewihr and when the war was over, Pascal, who had a mind for all things mechanical, would work in the shop and someday it would be his ...

Then Pascal Laurent sighed. "May I say something without giving offense, my friend Albert?"

"Certainly."

"I do wish you had not stuck me."

When the Frenchman said that, it made Albert want to cry and that made him angry. It made him want to shout. He wanted to kill Pascal Laurent, save that he knew he had already done so.

"Now may I ask something?" Pascal said. "A favor, if you might."

"Yes," Albert said.

"Can you pray for me?" He coughed and it was a very bad cough. "Will you pray for me?"

Albert said, "Pascal Laurent, listen to me, I will pray for you and I will pledge to you that when this is all over—the war, I mean—I will go to your Arleta and tell her that you died bravely and well for your country and I will ... I will somehow get money and it will be given to her so that she does not want ..."

"I feel I must interrupt ..." Pascal Laurent said weakly.

"Can you forgive me? Will you forgive me?" Albert Glucklich said.

Pascal Laurent tried to speak. He gurgled instead. It was very loud outside the crater and there was no question that a furious bombardment was being met with a no less furious counter-bombardment; still Albert could hear the gurgle and hear what it meant.

Albert Glucklich prayed. He said an *Ave Maria* and a *Pater*

Noster for Pascal Laurent whose body was pierced with the saw tooth bayonet of Albert Glucklich and he prayed a prayer for himself and then, maybe because he was not wholly sane then, he sang a little song he had learned when he was a child that was almost like a prayer that went:

> *In Japan boys sleep dreaming of silkworms*
> *And the boys of France dream of big fat snails*
> *And the boys in Russia dream of fur hats and blini*
> *But German lads dream of God and Fatherland*
> *German boys live and die*
> *for God and Fatherland ...*

On 11 November 1918 an armistice was signed. That war was over. The Germans did not win.

It was the not untoward fortune of Albert Glucklich to survive the war with all his limbs and senses, and unlike many men who say things in war and then forget them or try to, our Albert sought to honor his pledge.

He went to France and with no great difficulty found Arleta, the widow of Pascal Laurent, and he told her he had known her husband only briefly but liked him, liked him a great deal. You see, they had become friends, the very best of friends, under circumstances most trying, and now, Albert Glucklich meant to do whatever he could so that the wife of his dear friend would know no want.

The widow Laurent was a sweet-faced woman and one not given to asking questions that might confuse issues or her. She was a woman of strong likes and quick.

She very quickly came to like Albert Glucklich and when the time came that no one might deem it improper, Arleta married Albert Glucklich. If our Albert felt the need for confession, it was to his priest and not his wife.

While our Albert did not always learn quickly, what he learned it seemed he knew forever, and so it was that for many years after that war and many years after another, Albert Glucklich sold and repaired bicycles. He and Arleta visited Chicago in 1934 and dined at the Berghoff. For relaxation, Albert taught himself to play harmonica and joined a first-class amateur harmonica quartet that won third prize in a Hohner sponsored competition in Berlin in 1937. Arleta and Albert had four children, two sons and two daughters, who all survived surprisingly well the war that began in 1939 and the events that followed.

To his last confession and last rites, Albert Glucklich remained a steadfast and prayerful man, and he never forgot to thank God for all his good fortune and for his saw tooth bayonet.

THE COUNSELOR

I am a counselor. I help with problems: stress management, self-esteem, issues related to aging and illness, all the myriad difficulties of mental and emotional health.

My vocation is challenging. I am good at it. I treat it seriously. It is a sacred calling.

In mid-September, Darby Hillison calls me.

Darby Hillison, a former "counselor"—prior to his retirement, he'd been in the academic advising department of Elvera Community College—needs counseling. There's no irony intended in my remarking that. From time to time, all of us need "objective input" presented with "empathic listening," need someone to vent and rant to, need friend, spouse, clergyman, shaman or shrink to provide sympathetic ear or cluck-clucking tongue or "cut the bullshit" or "you're avoiding the issue" or hearty pat on the back or heartier kick in the ass.

I arrive at midnight. That is often the time we visit a client, though it's not a hard and fast rule: Midnight is the balance point between day and night. But counselors are flexible. If you need to meet me at 2:38 P.M. in the lobby of the Red Roof Inn on Butterfield Road in Downer's Grove or by the bank of dryers at LaunDRYland in Lincoln, Nebraska, that is fine, as long as it will enable us to get the job done.

The house is an older ranch, with aging vinyl siding; a cracked concrete drive leads to the attached garage.

There's the sudden illumination of a yellow bug light and Darby Hillison is at the door.

DARBY HILLISON

I ask him in. I do not *welcome* him. I do not want his company. I need his counseling. I know that.

I still think of this place as "our" house, Anna Belle's and mine. We own it. I don't think anyone actually plans to pay off a mortgage, not nowadays. Perhaps our generation is the last to establish that goal. A ceremony: We even burned the mortgage, but because we had no fireplace, we did it on the Weber kettle.

Our house.

Our generation.

My house. *My* generation.

It is no longer *Anna Belle* and *Darby* though I know that is how friends still think of us. Forgive the melodrama of my loneliness.

I miss her. I think maybe she could have helped me get through this, my Anna Belle ...

On her birth certificate, it's only *Anna*. She informally added *Belle* because she liked it two years after we were married in 1966. I liked it, too. She was Anna Belle.

Strange how loss can come upon you: One day Anna Belle awoke not feeling well. This was right after my retirement from Elvera. She felt quite bad and weak and so dizzy that it was almost as though her legs wouldn't hold onto the Earth and that she might float off ... All right, she actually said it, said she felt like she was *dying*. Anna Belle had a poetic nature but was not given to hyperbole. She scared me, and I was telling myself it was impossible that she could die. She needed to see a doctor and quickly.

We'd get into the Toyota Camry and I would drive her to Chadbourne County Hospital, to the emergency room. It was only eighteen miles. I was in control. I was not panicked. I was a good driver. Goddamn it, I was a good driver. I *am* a good driver.

No, she said she was too *gone*—that is the word she used— even for that, so I dialed 911 and the EMTs came in the firehouse ambulance and as they were getting her into it she said very fluttery "Oh, my" and they tried to help, they were fine young people and they knew what they were doing—I think I might even have advised one of them at Elvera some years back—but it turned out that the last words of my wife Mrs. Anna Belle Hillison were "Oh, my." It was a burst abdominal aortic aneurysm.

It is the kind of thing that can "just happen." So many things can just happen. If you ever really stop to think about all things that can *just happen*, you would go catatonic or lie whimpering under your blankets. You could go nowhere, do nothing.

The counselor sits down. I sit down. The counselor looks at me. I look around the room. There are pictures of friends' and relatives' children on the wall and the shelves. They are not our children. Anna Belle and I could not have kids.

The woman who has my position in the advising department at Elvera CC has a digital picture frame. An endless slide show like that, on what used to be my desk, it is a little disturbing, you know, like nothing is meant to stay still, nothing meant to stay as it was.

The counselor asks, "How are you?"

"All right," I say.

The counselor says nothing and blinks slowly, as though giving me a signal: *one-two-three.*

"Not so good."

The counselor nods.

"No good."

"I understand," the counselor says.

What he says is not just words. I can hear that.

Anna Belle used to read *Guideposts*, used to subscribe. There was a *Guideposts* poem she used to quote sometimes:

> *I listen not just to your words*
> *but to what makes you say them*
> *and me listen*

The counselor cants forward, hands out, as though taking a measurement. "It is six months."

It is six months and three days.

I tell him, "I need to talk."

"I know."

"About the girls," I say.

"Yes," The Counselor says.

This is the way we are put together, we normal ones. If the toothache of its own accord stops pounding with pain for more than a moment, we have to jab away at it with the tip of our tongue to set it throbbing once more.

"The girls," I say. "We must talk about them again."

THE GIRLS

Once there were four girls, BFF, and now there is one, Jessi Lynn Campbell, and she has a limp, although after two surgeries and three times a week therapy, it is much less pronounced. It is not impossible this disability will eventually vanish, or become perceptible only when she is extremely tired. Jessi Lynn has told her psychologist she is not certain she really wants to lose the limp, because—it's strange, somehow—that would be for her the irrevocable ending of the other three girls or at least the group identity they created and shared.

> *There are some things you have to let go of. You have to move on. That's the bullshit they give you.*
> *No, thank you, I don't think so, I do not think so.*
> *Utterly bogus. You lose your iPhone, okay, you let go of it, it's just a fucking phone. Your hamster dies and after a while you don't care because all it means is there's no squeaky exercise wheel waking you up at three in the morning.*

But Jessi Lynn has lost ...
BFF:

1.   Torme Bannings: red-headed and six feet one in height, maybe a tad more, and constantly pushed toward basketball (and weren't those coaches hearing "Go, Big Red!" and seeing trophies, but *Uh-uh—no way-es imposible!"* Torme suffered from an overactive klutz gland. Back when they were all in kindergarten, the teacher always made Torme sit on the floor because that way she was "not likely to fall off." Most improper to say something like that, of course, ever so much potential damage to self-esteem. But Torme—no exaggeration—from very early on, got along quite well with herself. She knew she'd always be the tallest and the gawkiest, a spastic flamingo, knew her hair would get attention which she could either choose to accept or

try to run from—and given her (non-)coordination she'd probably break both ankles. So she learned to laugh at herself, and, if you can do that, you can handle almost anything.

Funny, though, Torme was good *at riding a bicycle. The rest of us still had training wheels and there she was, zooming all over the place. God, don't you hate irony?*

2.   Velma Sheffield: Bold Venture Velma, rock-climber and rappeller, snorkeler and skier, surfer and snowboarder. Velma the Extreme. She rode English and even with the helmet, one time when she got tossed on her head—BONK!—she saw double for two weeks, but hey, a life that's not lived is a life you're not *living,* and so as soon as the doctors said "Concussion free and good to go" she was out there jumping. Velma was cute as hell, blondicious cheerleader cute, check out that itty-bitty nose and it's genetic not rhinoplastic, and no call for orthodonture on those pearly whites. And she was smart, smart as hell, 35 on the ACT, and she had boy friends, but they were more *friends* and she was so vivacious and up and out there—a little overwhelming for high school guys, to tell the truth, so there just weren't any romantic romances.

The Girl Gang … If Velma was there for you, she was 110% *there* for you. Always.

Funny, I'm saying it figures it was Velma who came up with a bicycle trip, a "senior rite of passage" (ride of passage?) and that makes sense, because Velma was the one who made stuff happen, but … I've got it in my mind that it was all of us made the decision. It was like group think. Gestalt.

3.   Mary Smith. Most American of us all, and happy to be so, and she was in her church (Methodist) youth group and played piano ("Für Elise" and "Raindrops (Keep Falling on my Head)" her favorites) and liked to bake (cookies with twice the recipe's chocolate chips) and always took Cosmo the Lakeland terrier for a walk. Mary Smith was adopted as an infant and John and Alice Smith, her adoptive parents, had flown to Ethiopia to get her and

when the time came that she could ask why she was so dark and they were nearly transparent, they explained the situation and they must have done a fine job of it because something in her reverberated in affirmation of all that could be offered by the USA. She believed in God. She believed in Obama. She believed in hard work. She earned money babysitting. She supported the troops. She had perfect attendance every year except for seventh grade when she had mono. She and her mother watched *Old Yeller* once a year to cry and *A Christmas Story* to laugh.

> *You know what gets me crying sometimes, I mean, the worst fucking kind of crying?* Mary Smith. *Mary was just so goddamn nice. And I don't mean the horseshit fakey nice that makes you reach for your insulin. She was just the nicest goddamn person. She was* grateful *for life. She was abundantly grateful.*

These were good kids. Two of them seventeen, two eighteen, all seniors at Prairie-Way. They were mature in the right way (not cynical and snottified). If their lives were shaped by privilege, they were also laden with promise. No backstory here, no addictions or self-asphyxiations, no bullying or bulimia, no cutting, purging, unprotected sex, no suicide attempts and few thoughts of death beyond the abstract, the metaphysical, the ageless wondering of adolescents (and everyone else): *Where do we go from here?* No gossip grist and gristle for *The View, Larry King, Wolf Blitzer*, the Fox Network.

Not a cliché: Everybody loved them.

Once there were four girls.

Now three are dead.

THE BICYCLE TRIP

A Spring Break trip. New bicycles? Well, a decent bike, a Marin Portofina or a BikeHard LadyCruz, you're looking at 500 to 800 bucks, but it's something they'll take to college, and it will last for years; it's not frivolous or faddish. Southern Illinois. Spring hits earlier down there than the northern part of state. Everything's green. There's rolling land and lakes and Shawnee National Forest and the town of Makanda inhabited by artists and artisans and leathery unreconstructed hippies and site of the annual VultureFest (Groovy! Look it up in your Funk and Wagnall's—that is, Wikipedia).

And they'd planned it carefully. While it's been proven the average American high schooler could not find the Grand Canyon if you dropped him into it with a GPS super-glued to his head and an iPad stuck to his ass, the girls consulted Messrs. Rand and McNally, mapped out scenic routes ...

But, come on, you're talking kids here—and, say, maybe I'm old-fashioned, but girls *at that, four girls traveling through, among other places, Williamson County, known for historical reason as "Bloody Williamson," and Nile City, aka the Midwest's Merry Meth Capital. The world is not what it used to be, you know, you hear all kinds of things ...*

Sure do. You will notice, *s'il vous plaît*, these kids have heads under their bicycle helmets. That's why they asked Jessi Lynn's very own personal *father*, Mr. James D. Campbell, DDS, to chaperone them.

He was flattered. He was due a vacation. He had family in Southern Illinois, had fished and boated in the summer at Lake Benton. So he'd drive along with 'em, cell phone and visual contact, roger that, and he'd try to stay out of their way when they wanted him to ...

FROM THE SOUTHERN ILLINOIS HERALD

... according to police, the sixty-eight-year-old driver, Darby Hillison of Thomsville, veered across a rural stretch of highway in southern Illinois and collided with the four bicyclists, killing ...

... maintained that his 2004 Toyota Camry suddenly accelerated, causing him to lose control and cross the center line ... no evidence of drug or alcohol impairment ... safe driving record ... cited for improper lane usage ...

... were pronounced dead at the scene ... ruptured spleen and sheered socket of the right hip, she is expected to make a full recovery ...

THE COUNSELOR

Darby Hillison says, "It is not my fault."

I say nothing.

"So whose fault is it?" Darby Hillison says. "Toyota's? God Himself?"

Is this about assigning blame? The police cited him only for a minor traffic violation; there were no criminal charges filed. The mother of Mary Smith—Dear God, *Mary Smith!*—said at her child's funeral that she knew Mary would have forgiven him because that was what Christ taught and she ...

Blame does not have to exist.

There *can* be accountability.

Three children are dead.

Their families can never fully heal, can never be made whole.

That's what matters.

That and what Darby Hillison feels in the depths of his heart, in his lonely house, in the silences of the long nights.

Darby Hillison is utterly still for a heavy, contemplative moment. I am here. He knows he has my support.

Then he tells me what he intends to do.

DARBY HILLISON

Darby Hillison is behind the wheel of the Toyota Camry. He starts the engine. Cars today, oh, they don't make 'em like they used to. Now, cars always start, no matter if it's raining or the temperature hits twenty below. The motor is a soft purr, so smooth and so quiet.

You can count on Toyota.

And he rolls his window down.

And he leans back in the comfortable driver's seat.

And after a while, his eyes close.

And you might think he is drifting off to sleep, there at the wheel of his car inside his garage, but he is drifting away, losing consciousness.

He is dying, is what he is doing.

And then after not very long a time, Darby Hillison is dead.

THE COUNSELOR

I am a counselor.
I help with problems.
I set things right.

THE OVAL PORTRAIT

Edgar Allan Poe, born January 19, 1809, Boston, Massachusetts, died October 7, 1889, Giverny, France.
– Wikipedia

Genius is immediate, but talent takes time. Genius or talent or neither, the literary world remains divided about the efforts of Edgar Allan Poe III, but public has rendered a verdict: Last year, Poe's novel *Eldorado* outsold Sabatini's *Mistress Wilding*, Zane Grey's *The Call of the Canyon*, and Booth Tarkington's *The Midlander*. Secretive about his work, Poe has revealed that his new novel is entitled *The Oval Portrait*; it will be published in March of next year by Grosset & Dunlap.
– "Letter from Paris"
– Genet
The New Yorker
April 11, 1925

It was the start of summer with weather more like spring and I was very poor and very happy because I was in Paris and had a woman who loved me, and many days the writing went well. The best work time was early morning when the shopkeepers were wetting down the streets and the smell of fresh bread was everywhere, but on this rare evening, I was writing with one of my stubby pencils at a small table outside the Lilas Café. I was writing well. Perhaps I did not yet have the one true sentence I needed that led to everything else, but I was stalking it, creeping up on that sentence.

Then I heard the café door behind me. I heard a huff and puff like a leaky steam engine and an unsteady shuffle and then I got the odor of him.

Ford Madox Ford, as he called himself then, greatly resembled Humpty-Dumpty prior to the great fall. He had a heavy, stained English mustache and wanted to be thought of as another G.K. Chesterton. Ford's watery eyes made it seem as though his whole face were beginning to dissolve. And the aroma he radiated was not that of a British man of letters.

"Might I sit?" he asked, as he sat down at my table.

Thus endeth the writing, I thought, *pues y nada.*

A moment to repent and digress: I am a journalist and I need render a more objective opinion of Ford Madox Ford than has been the case so far. Let it be said that in *The Good Soldier* our Mr. Ford wrote a good book. In fairness, let it also be said, he wrote a large number of bad ones. Let it be said that with the literary magazine the *transatlantic review* he championed innovative 20th century writing and 20th century writers, myself, let it be said, among them. Let it be said that he did much to encourage the *avant-garde* in all areas of the arts.

Let it also be said that he did so in order to have people to whom he might condescend.

No matter the Fordian virtues, he smelled. He smelled awfully bad.

And when he spoke to me over the small café tables you'd have thought his breath was the result of his kissing a goat.

"You were writing, Hem," he said.

"Was," I said.

He slapped my shoulder.

"That's the stuff."

"I'm just full of the stuff," I said.

"Let me buy you a drink," he said.

"I will allow you to," I said.

He waved over a waiter, a thin man with a frozen face. Ford Madox Ford did not condescend toward waiters. He was of that class of English society which did not notice servants at all. They were no more worthy of attention than a boot jack or a telephone.

Ford ordered a *fine à l'eau.* I had been drinking beer. I ordered a *fine à l'eau.*

"Hem, I have something for you, Hem."

"That's good, Ford Ford," I said. He disliked my chiding him about his assumed name. "Everybody likes something."

He gave me a queer look.

"You know Edgar Allan Poe," he said.

"The third," I said. "I do not know the Third, Ford Ford. I know of him."

And who did not know of Poe Three? His novels typically sold two million copies. In English. There were copies in other languages, perhaps even Urdu and Hottentot. There were motion pictures.

Everyone who worked at the scrivener's trade, Bartleby no doubt included, knew of Edgar Allan Poe III. We all applauded his success. Writers are a benevolent and big-hearted lot.

"You've read him, Hem?"

"A little," I said. I stopped halfway through the first chapter of *Eldorado.* I feared contagion.

"I would like to publish a profile of Edgar Allan Poe III in the *transatlantic review.* I would like you to write it."

I sighed.

"You know, Hem. Does he think of himself as American or French? How does he consider his literary heritage ...?"

I said, "Does he drink? Does he use opium? Does he smoke *Gitanes?* Has he had an affair with Isadora Duncan or Josephine Baker or both? Can he play the 'La Marseillaise' on the Jew's harp?"

"You have a sense of humor, Hem."

"It is a gift."

"I liked that profile you did of Mussolini for the Toronto Daily Star. It had wit. 'There is something wrong, even histrionically, with a man who wears white spats with a black shirt.'" Ford chuckled. He sounded tubercular.

"Mussolini is quite the comic, Ford Ford."

Ford offered me one hundred and fifty dollars and I agreed to write a profile of Edgar Allan Poe III.

Then Ford left and I took my pencil and wrote a true sentence. Ford Madox Ford is an ass.

The weather remained beautiful as Scott Fitzgerald and I set out to motor to Giverny. The top was down but we had it if needed because Scott had replaced the top on the Renault KJ although Zelda had not wanted him to do so: Zelda thought a topless boat tailed Renault would add to the Fitzgerald image as American eccentrics. Zelda also thought herself a master chef because she could mix vinegar and oil in nearly the right proportions for salad. Zelda thought herself a writer and she thought herself a dancer. Zelda thought herself herself herself.

I liked Scott. Though I never said it to him, there are things you do not speak of, Scott was the least conceited, most talented writer I ever knew, which made him endearing and quite sad. Zelda used his humility to humiliate him and sucked away at his talent until he could only write bad stories for *The Saturday Evening Post* and worse movies for Hollywood.

Zelda did not like me. I did not like Zelda. Scott said she was "the first American flapper," but Zelda belonged to another breed: Zelda Sayre Fitzgerald was a vampire, a vamp, à la Theda Bara, the *femme fatale* who drains her victim and leaves him either a shambling ruin or a corpse.

It was to give Scott respite from Zelda that I suggested he accompany me on my trip to profile *Monsieur* Poe. I drove. Scott did not like to drive drunk and he had begun to drink even before we left Paris. He had his engraved hip flask: *To 1st Lt. F. Scott Fitzgerald. 65th Infantry. Camp Sheridan . Forget-me-not. Zelda. 9-13-18.*

Zelda could work him even at a distance.

"Old Overholt," Scott said, offering the whiskey. I took a small drink. The Renault was a pretty whore of a car. It looked beautiful but was no good inside. The three-speed manual transmission was from the days before the war and the brakes worked only on the rear wheels. It was the kind of car you could drive more easily if you were a little drunk.

"Hem, you are my friend. You are my good friend."

"I am."

"Then may I ask you a question?"

There was whiskey in Scott's words, each syllable a bit too crisp so he would not sound like he was slurring. I feared what he would ask.

"Are you afraid to die, Hem?"

"I have been," I said.

"I am," Scott said.

"At some times, more than other times. In the war, you know, I was often afraid to die. Then came the time I was blown up and felt my spirit leave me then snap back to me." I held out my hand for the flask. "Since then, I have not been so much afraid to die."

"Hem," Scott said, "I saw him again yesterday."

"Oh," I said.

When he said nothing more, I prompted: "And who might he be, friend Scott?"

Scott sighed. "That spectre in my path. My demonic brother. The very apparition of Francis Scott Key Fitzgerald, Esquire."

"Someone who looks like you ..."

"Exactly. I left the flat and there he was, across the way, by the Tilsitt street sign. He was wearing my jacket, this jacket I have on now, and he waved to me. And just before I fully recognized him, he stepped round the corner and disappeared."

"So you saw someone who looked like you ..."

"A doppelgänger, Hem."

"Doppelgänger. That sounds like some type of German pervert. A man who does obscene things with sausages."

"It is not funny, Hem."

His pain was not funny.

"The doppelgänger is your exact double. And meeting him ... It's a harbinger of death. Hem, I am going to die. I don't want to die."

"Have you seen your doppelgänger before, Scott?"

"This was the third time. Once, when I was young. At Princeton. Then New York, the morning of my wedding. It was just outside St. Patrick's."

"Consider, Scott. You saw him twice previous. After each occurrence, you evidently did not die."

"That is true," Scott said. "It's true." He thought about that.

"Drink more, Scott."

"That won't help."

"It won't hurt," I said.

He drank more and it must have given him insight, because he did not talk about death or doppelgängers the rest of the way to Giverny.

From "Poe III"
A Profile of the Artist
by Ernest Hemingway

There are some secrets which do not permit
themselves to be told.
– Edgar Allan Poe (I)

... gardens of Edgar Allan Poe's home are neither as
ordered as those of his neighbor Renoir nor as
natural as Monet's, but there is the feeling of
exploding wildness under stern control. There are
beds of Hybrid Tea roses and Mexican yucca, along
with wild grasses and cattails. And of course, as we
stepped over the pond on the arched Japanese
bridge, we observed the water lilies. In the summer
bloom, the myriad scents invoke the strange
lushness of prehistoric wood and swamp.

Scott and I were led by Poe and two quite attractive
albeit exceedingly pale young women, identified
only as, "my dear companions," to an arbor, where
we sat at a rustic table.

Poe's smile surprises, in that he so strongly
resembles his grandfather, someone thought of as "a
man of sorrowful visage." Poe has an expansive
forehead and deep set eyes, and while his mustache
is pencil thin in the manner of a cinema
swashbuckler and his hair of moderate length, it is
easy to imagine a daguerreotype of Grandfather Poe
come to life.

The two young women left us, to return shortly with
a bottle of Moët & Chandon and the proper service,
along with an assortment of pastries: the upside-
down *tarte Tatin, petit fours*, angel wings, *bichon au
citron, Gâteau la broche* and *madeleines*. They
waited on us in silence.

Then Poe toasted: "To dreams within dreams." There
was something false and scornful that lay beneath
his pleasant tone.

To begin, I inquired of his taste in literature. Of the

moderns, he likes Edgar Rice Burroughs and Edna Ferber. Of the classics, he has a mild fondness for Hawthorne but finds him too moralistic. His late father, Poe the II, he praises for his boldness in exploring psychological manias and fears, and of course, his grandfather rests on his majestic throne atop literature's Mt. Olympus. He did not say that in acquiring the themes and style of his forebear Mr. Poe has inherited a gold mine.

Hypothetical question: If Poe had not left the USA for France, might ...

Poe interrupted me. "But he did, my dear Mr. Hemingway." He laughed the way Ford Madox Ford laughs.

"And doesn't everyone know *that* story."

Washington College Hospital
The Tower, Second Floor
Sunday, October 7, 1849
4:30 A.M.

Semiconscious, he mutters and shrieks in anguished delirium. Does Edgar Allan Poe— Poe, Southern gentleman, critic, devoted husband, poet, drunkard, author, editor, and by his own admission, genius—call to friend, foe, or phantasm as he thrashes on what must surely be his deathbed? Following his simultaneous bouts of drinking and profound melancholia, Poe has been diagnosed as suffering from "brain fever," perhaps exacerbated by a stout knock or two on the noggin.

Nobody quite knows what brain fever was, but it seems to have killed many people until early in the 20th century at which time the scientific community jettisoned the term as too vague to even aspire to meaninglessness. Delirium and hallucinations and, of course, high fevers, were symptomatic of brain fever and no question, our Eddie is utterly deranged.

—Is that you, Doctor?

He sees someone at his bedside. Dr. Moran has been kind to him, admitted him to hospital, though Dr. Moran, like many of Poe's acquaintance, knows he stands little chance of being paid.

Alas, Poe is King Midas in reverse: All that he touches turns to shite.

—God have mercy on my poor soul, Poe says.

"Not all that likely, Edgar." There is a laughing whisper.

—Moran?

"Not all that likely, Edgar."

—Then who?

The voyeur at the bedside of the ill-favored and sore beset Edgar Allan Poe smiles.

—Ah, says Poe. Your smile—it is my smile!

"Oh, Eddie, Eddie, as now you stand before the veil, please acknowledge me at last, call me by name."

—You are, Poe declares, William Wilson.

"Please, Mr. Poe, might you not leave off the fictions when you will soon know the eternities of Truth and the truth of Eternity?

"Edgar, once you wrote a story entitled ... Why, yes, you called that tale 'William Wilson,' and it is begun thusly:

"'*Let me call myself, for the present, William Wilson. The fair page now lying before me need not be sullied with my real appellation.*'

"But that story was hardly a creation of your lauded Poetic Imagination but rather ... autobiography!"

The dying man thinks he is being punished as the doleful interrogation continues: "Who am I, Mr. Edgar Allan Poe?"

—You are ... the man in the mirror. You are that spectre in my path. You are, oh, my double, my brother ... MYSELF!

"Though your brains have been slow-cooked and your innards pickled in alcohol, you yet possess your ratiocinative ability, Mr. Poe. How many times throughout your four decades upon this mortal sphere have you seen me, your doppelgänger? I was the near perfect *imitation* of you, in words and actions: Oh, you must commend me for how admirably did I play my part. I followed your manner of dress: threadbare and fallen far from fashion, yet you had a certain style, particularly the cape. Your gait, the unbalanced drunkard's lurch or the stride of an arrogant Southern gentleman, and your raving idiosyncrasies were, without difficulty, appropriated. Even your voice did not escape me. I can emote as well as you, Eddie, lad: 'Once upon a midnight dreary. I speak blah-blah-blah and quoth the raven, Nevermore, blah-blah-blah and Nevermore ...'

"On so many occasions, Edgar, I have been *mistaken* for you. On so many occasions, my rudeness and lewdness and foolishness were accredited to *you*. When I doused myself with laudanum and *spiritus frumenti* and roared of angels crawling up my arse or bells that would not cease their dread tolling, or hearts that beat endlessly on though their—owners—had been hacked to bits, I was by many thought to be you. And you, at the time, more often than not, were snoring in foul slumber brought on by crude gin or opium.

"Edgar, I confess without apology: For much that you were blamed and disdained and stigmatized and even ostracized in this life, I am the one responsible. As your reputation declined, you sought solace in alcohol or drugs, further diminishing yourself, allowing me to drain from you all your qualities, such as they were. And now you are so dissipated, so diminished, I will take what little remains."

Dying, Poe asks:

—O my double, O my brother of unease, are you Death?

A laugh.

"Death is death. As for me, I do not know my origin. I live upon the energies of others,

sapping their vital source, much like the Greek vampires feast upon blood. But I need nothing as coarse as bodily fluids to sustain me. I drain the very soul and the very self, at first little by little, and then ...

"I become what I behold.

"I am like unto you and now, now that you have weakened your will so that you can no longer hold steadfastly onto your essence, the uniqueness and singularity of Edgar Allan Poe, I will take *all* that you are and were and could have been and I shall become ... Edgar Allan Poe!"

—No, Poe says, a feeble protest. I do not wish to die.

"There we have a fitting inscription for every headstone since time began. But, if you will, Eddie, if you will grant the metaphysical truth of irony and metaphor, you will not die at all.

"You will live forever.

"I will see to that!"

—Please ...

And now with a bow all the more infuriating because of its delicately mannered courtesy, the spectre pulled forth an envelope from the interior of his jacket and took from it a thrice folded sheet of stationery. "This letter is addressed to you, Eddie, but I have the greater use for it." He chuckled without mirth. "It is … Ha! A purloined letter!" Then he began to read aloud, with perhaps just a hint of a sardonic French accent:

My Dear Monsieur Poe,

Please allow me to confess that upon first receiving copies of your work from the French publisher *Poulet-Malassis*, who inquired as to the possibility of my translating your stories and poems into French, and my noting that you were both American born and for the most part American educated, I presumed I might find little to excite or even interest me: I expected gross sentiment and cliché and nothing that might be judged *original*. The weak twig that is America has not yet had a chance to grow far from the tree of Europe. But truth be told, the translation of genius or doggerel would yet produce for me a few francs by which I might sustain myself, and so I read your stories with growing wonder and astonishment.

Please accept my apology, my dear M.E. A. Poe, as I humbly bow before your genius.

I read "The Black Cat" and "Mesmeric Revelation," and dashed the manuscripts to the floor, in awe and dismay, asking the walls, "How is it possible for this man to have written *my* stories before I've had the opportunity to do so?"

You left me dazed and weeping upon my chaise.

I will translate your work, and feel myself at a sacred task, honored with each word, each comma. This is what I told the publisher.

Mr. Poe, forgive my audacity, but I strongly sense a spiritual kinship with you. Mr. Poe, we are brothers. We understand whisperings at the edge of darkness and flowers of alluring evil. We know that the forlorn echo of a single word can ring throughout the ages and evoke the unspeakable even as it calls forth rare beauty.

But I do not flatter myself. I am the younger brother, a dullard and lackwit, who dares to hope I might know some small illumination from your brilliance. I beg for the chance to learn what my poor intellect might absorb from you. Mr. Poe, dare I hope you could teach me, become my *maître à penser*?

Moreover, Mr. Poe, I feel forced to speak of matters practical. I know you have endured sorrows and hardships in the United States. You have been cruelly used by critics and deceived by false friends. You have seldom enjoyed the popular success that ought to be afforded one of your rare gifts.

I am determined, my dear Monsieur Poe, that you will became as renowned in France as you should be in the United States. With no chauvinism, I can state that my country will welcome and applaud you and award you the laurels to which you are entitled.

Thus, though I am hardly a man of means, I will arrange for your passage to France, and should you accede to this request to come here, I will do all that I might on your behalf.

Please do respond soon, my American brother, and trust that I am your dear friend and most fervent admirer,

– Charles Baudelaire

According to Dr. John Joseph Moran, Edgar Allan Poe died at 5:00 A.M., October 8, 1949.

A funeral was conducted the next day at the Presbyterian cemetery at Fayette and Green Streets. The weather was cold and exceedingly damp and threatened to grow worse. Only eight people attended as Poe's rude pine coffin, lacking handles or even a pillow for his head, went into the grave.

On the following Monday, October 16, at four in the afternoon, a disheveled man presented himself at Washington College Hospital and asked to see Dr. John Joseph Moran. When the Moran came forth, physician's eyes grew large and his jaw dropped. To prevent himself from fainting, he dropped into a chair, murmuring, "As I live and breathe ..."

"As do I," interrupted the visitor.

KNOWING WHEN TO DIE

"Edgar Allan Poe!"

"I fear, Dr. Moran, your diagnosis of my death was inaccurate. And I fear my burial was all too premature."

"I ... I do not understand."

"Nor need you. You have the evidence before you. If you visit the Presbyterian cemetery, you shall have the further corroboration of my empty grave."

At this, Dr. Moran was afforded a courtly bow and his visitor departed.

Originally published in the Philadelphia *Dollar Newspaper* in 1844, Poe's short story, "The Premature Burial" became wildly popular throughout the United States and was reprinted in dozens of newspapers and literary journals along with an account of how the author himself had suffered the fate of the title and survived.

In the first week of December, Mrs. Maria Clemm, Poe's aunt who had also been his mother-in-law, received a letter:

> My Dear Muddy,
> It is with regret that I must bid you *adieu*, the woman who has so succored me and sought to support me in all my efforts.
> For me, this country will always be a realm of torturing memories and dread, of limitless sorrow for which there is no balm in Gilead nor Baltimore nor Richmond.
> I have been given another chance.
> I have been born again.
> I leave you with my eternal love as the new Edgar Allan Poe seeks to find fortune and himself in the Old World.
> Farewell, my dearest Muddy and you will dwell forever in my heart.
> Yours Most Sincerely,
> Eddie

Mrs. Clemm never heard from him again.

Like his (wrongly) celebrated *père* and his even more

(wrongly) celebrated *grand-père,* Edgar Allan Poe III has been (wrongly) praised for the musicality of his writing, and indeed, his novel *The Oval Portrait* is a song: An interminable lullaby. A soporific symphony. Poe has not met the adjective or adverb he did not like, nay, adore, nay VENERATE!!!—all of them employed in coma-causing fashion from which the reader can only be revivified, or at least brought back to eye open catatonia, by Poe's frequent use of the exclamation point.

I have done Poe the service of stealing a number of his exclamation points, though I doubt he will notice. Take them, and use them sparingly, or better still, not at all.

!!!!!!!!!!!!!!!!!!!! !!!!!!!!!!!!!!!!!!!

Buried beneath awkward arabesque phrases and whirligigs of words, there is a plot which, on occasion, if you are quick enough, might be discerned in this alleged novel. It is a plot that plods plods e'er so pokily: An artist, Adolpho Maillard, paints portraits of lovely young women and men, all of whom die, as he drains their "life essence, spirit and soul ..."

This is the premise of Grampy Poe's short story, likewise entitled "The Oval Portrait," a story which is a merciful two pages. Yes, III has exploited birthright rather than creativity.

In his "Oval Portrait," Poe Number One writes: "Long, long I read—and devoutly, devotedly I gazed."

And to close this review, I write: "Long, long I read — and numbly and dumbly I glazed over by page 38."

As will you, Dear Reader.

Delwyn Shay
The Farringford Review of Books
March, 1926

Universal Pictures has purchased the rights to *The Oval*

Portrait by Edgar Allan Poe III for a reputed six figures. German Expressionist master Paul Leni is set to direct, with William Haines and Charles Farrell in contention for the starring role of Adolpho Maillard and the "Green-eyed Goddess of Hollywood" Jane Winton as leading lady.

    – *Variety*

    ... Poe became an icon of first French and then world literature. He died at his home in Giverny in 1889, lionized by artists of every medium.

    – Wikipedia

A Brief Epilogue

F. Scott Fitzgerald, born September 24, 1896, in St. Paul, Minnesota, died, September, 20, 1970, Los Angeles, California, abandoned novel writing at the end of the 1930s to write popular short stories, screenplays, and TV scripts until his death. He was a contributor to Rod Serling's influential *Twilight Zone*, nominated for an Emmy for his script, "The Doppelgänger," and shared film credits with Jack Finney and Daniel Mainwaring for the 1956 film *The Invasion of the Body Snatchers.*

Summing up his career in an interview in *Playboy* in 1969, Fitzgerald said, "I'd say there are second acts in American lives."

    – Wikipedia

"Boy, was that a dream, or was it!"
– Johnny, protagonist of *Robot Monster*

Prologue

ROBOT MONSTER: A guy in a gorilla suit and diving helmet portrays Ro-Man, who has come from outer space (or possibly our moon) to destroy all the inhabitants of Earth. Film critic Leonard Maltin described the 1953 film as "one of the genuine legends of Hollywood; embarrassingly, hilariously awful." It was directed by Phil Tucker, with a screenplay by Wyott Ordung.

DREAMING ROBOT MONSTER

OUR CAST

JOHNNY: Eight years old. Slap him a good one and Child Welfare won't call it abuse.

CARLA: Johnny's younger sister, five or six years of premeditated cuteness.

ALICE: Johnny's older sister. Stacked. When she becomes a scientist in Johnny's dream, you don't buy it. Not with a rack like that.

MOM: Mom has problems not even hinted at in the film. (When the films of all of our lives are produced, I think this will also be said of us.)

THE PROFESSOR: *Claims* to be an archaeologist. Commie? Note the accent.

ROY: The Professor's assistant. Quite good looking. *Too* good looking, if you catch my drift.

RO-MAN: Space Alien from the planet Ro-Man, according to Johnny.

THE GREAT GUIDANCE: Ro-man's boss, leader of the Ro-men. As seen on television.

ALICE

Robot Monster was not a robot. That is a misconception. That was the name Johnny, my obnox little brother, gave him, or really, what Johnny called the story.

> *ROBOT MONSTER! Credits roll over a background of violent science-fiction and gruesome and subversive horror comic books. Once every kid in the United States read comic books. Good kids read* Archie *and* Little Lulu *and* Walt Disney's Comics and Stories. *Then there were the rest of us.*

This explains a great deal.

Oh, he was not of our world. He was *Ro*-man, not *Hu*man—but he was *not* a monster.

He wasn't.

I know.

Alice sighs.

Robot Monster was my brother's dream.

But what of me? Have I no dreams?

I am eleven years older. Do my dreams matter less than those of a juvenile delinquent and socially warped OBNOX of an eight year old boy?

I

JOHNNY

Alice is smart, okay, reading books all the time. She's got big torpedoes and I don't care what she thinks, she is NOT the boss of me. I know Alice kissed Sidney Gerstein behind the garage. Sidney's a Jew with glasses and he's a sissy. The Italian guys three blocks over beat him up all the time. That's the kind of guy my sister kisses. A creep.

I tried to tell Mom about Alice and sissy Sidney, but, well, Mom is strange. She never gets mad, not really. You ask mom "How are you?" and she maybe says, "Hello" or "Tuesday" or "That's just fine." Mom, to tell the truth, is weirdsville. Not Daffy Duck weirdsville or Clarabelle Clown weirdsville. *Quiet* weirdsville. Very strange.

Some of the kids at Christ the Comforter say Mom is "like from outer space, man," and then they snap their fingers like beatniks and laugh. Bastards. Alice the Smart says I have to just ignore those "dolts who cannot appreciate or comprehend divergent thinking." Yeah, that's some kind of big tickle, all right. Alice is as full of good advice as a prune is full of pruneiness.

Smarty-smart Alice was not around when everything got started. It was me and Carla. I had my space helmet and Carla had her stupid doll.

(Robot monster got Carla, but that's later. It bothers me. Carla really wasn't all too bad. I don't know what happened to her doll.)

So we were out playing. Mom and Alice had taken us on a picnic somewhere you could call the Valley of Bad Shaped Rocks. It was the kind of place you go on picnics when you're dreaming crazy stuff.

We spread out this itchy old green army blanket on a place that didn't have any big rocks and was only a little bit lumpy. Mom said Dad brought the blanket home from the army. I know Dad was a soldier. Once he let me play with a cigar box full of ribbons and medals. They were neat. Then Dad started to cry for no reason and he hugged me and he didn't say anything and I said, "Men don't cry," and he said, "Jesus wept," which is what you figure one of the nuns at Christ the Comforter would say. Then Dad wrapped his long, long arms around me, and he told me to be quiet, just be quiet, and he said he loved me very much. Then he did his Mr. Monkey face with his lips all pooched out and eyes bugging and made the ape sound that's pretty funny even if doesn't sound too much like an ape.

Dad is dead now.

Mom made the usual for the picnic. Peanut butter and jelly sandwiches. Baloney sandwiches. We had Kool-Aid. Kool-Aid's cheaper than soda. Kool-Aid even tastes cheap.

Some fucking picnic, huh?

So then Carla and I go exploring, I guess you could call it, and I have my Captain Cosmos space helmet and my Zeta12 ray gun that shoots bubbles. Most of the kids at Christ the Comforter want to be cowboys like Hopalong Cassidy or Gene Autry or Roy Rogers. Cowboys are okay or even cool, is what the nuns think, and Sister Mary Loyola is always telling us about how she went to the *Catholic Charities Hour* radio show in New York and saw Bing

Crosby, Bishop Fulton J. Sheen, and Singing Cowboy Bob Atcher. This kid, Billy Svoboda, said he wanted to be Dale Evans and Mother Cordelia smacked him.

I don't know why nuns hate spacemen, but they do. Sometimes I think Jesus was a spaceman who landed here and got all messed up. Next time Jesus comes, He better bring an atomic ray gun.

The Valley of Bad Shaped rocks is bad news for picnics, but it's real good for SPACEMAN because it looks like Mars or some other outer space planet.

Of course Carla wants to play HOUSE.

I tell her no and shut up.

She goes sniffle-sniffle and I'm not sure if she is going to cry or if it's asthma because she's coming down with a rock allergy or something. She yaps some more that we have to play HOUSE.

I tell her to cast an eyeball on all the neat rocks. Cool, huh?

Carla says if I don't play HOUSE she will tell about that time in the bath tub.

I shoot some Zeta12 ray gun bubbles POP right in her eye and she yells and makes like she's going to cry but I tell her she better not so she doesn't but she tells me she hates me and I tell her ask me if I care. (Because I DON'T care. I don't care if everyone hates me. They can all go to hell, but first, let them just take one little minute to KISS my ASS!)

That's when we meet Roy and The Professor. They're at the entrance to a cave, chipping away at rocks.

Roy is young and he's got dynamic tension muscles like Charles Atlas (Charles ASSLESS, that's a joke) but Roy's hair is greasy-curly like he gave himself a Toni perm like a lady. Roy is pretty va-va-voom—if you can say that about a man.

The Professor is saggy with a turkey neck and turkey eyes. (What a turkey!) He turns into my dad (but that's later). He talks in a funny way that's like English but with something stuck on his back teeth and his throat. The way he sounds, well, he sounds like a Red. (But my dad, my real dad, wasn't any Commie.)

I tell them I want to blast them with my Zeta12. You can see they both think I'm just one cute little tyke, a regular little rascal, aw shucks, the bastards. The Professor tosses me this jive about Roy and him: "... archaeologists":

People who try to find out what men were like way

back before they could read or write. Then he tells me, wouldn't it be nicer if we could live at peace with each other?

Pinko, what'd I tell you? Uh-huh, that's Bolshevik boushwah. Commie prick.

(You go to Catholic school, by the time you're second grade with Sister Mary Loyola, you learn all about the Red Menace. They don't always have Jewish names, either. Communists hate Catholics. Communists torture priests and rape nuns and kill little kids before their first communion. Then kids go to Limbo because of the fucking Communists. That's how it works.)

Then Mom and Alice show up. You can never know if Mom's upset. It's usually like someone's gone over her brain with Johnson's wax (Stay tuned for "The Mom from Outer Space" on the same channel!), but Alice is definitely bent out of shape, because ... Carla and I were supposed to take a NAP right after lunch!

(See what I mean about this picnic? A NAP? Give me a break.)

Roy gives Alice the once-over and then the twice-over. Maybe he likes her. Or maybe he's worried she's prettier than he is.

Then, or in just a little bit, Ro-man destroys the earth—pretty much, anyway.

II
MOM

Before I drowned, when I was a little girl, I was really quite wild. Yes, I was. It was like my mind was carbonated, filled with this frantic loud and wet buzzing that spread downward, made me vibrate and tingle with wicked energy. And grownups would speak to me, they would always tell me what to do, and I would maybe not quite understand, maybe, I don't know why, but I would maybe get the *idea* of what they were telling me to do— and then I would *buzz-buzz- buzz not* do it and would instead *buzz-buzz-buzz* do the direct opposite, if there was a direct opposite, and if not, I might do something slantwise or catty-corner or at the least, different.

Go to bed now, Mother said, and I took the box of kitchen

matches and set the bed on fire and got so close to it that my hair burned. It made a sound that I can think of sometimes but cannot quite hear.

I would sing a song backwards and very loud then, if Uncle Peter or someone asked me to stop, I would start screaming and I could not even stop myself from screaming until I hit someone or bit myself.

Once I tore all the shades from the windows because the spring rollers made this twangy noise that made me laugh and my father picked me up and slapped me on the legs and shoulders and the back of my head all the way down the hall and threw me into the front closet and locked it and I ripped all the clothes from the hangers and peed on the whole pile with that twanging noise inside my head inside my head inside my head.

But then one day we went on a picnic. I still like picnics very much. If you ask me to go on a picnic, why, I will make peanut butter and jelly sandwiches and I will make baloney sandwiches and I will fill thermos bottles with Cherry Kool-Aid and Grape Kool-Aid and Orange Kool-Aid and we will just go on a picnic, that is what.

The picnic when I drowned was a picnic with my mother and father and Uncle Peter and Aunt Alma and all my cousins and there was beer and a portable radio with Hank Williams and softball and sweet humming mosquitoes and the smell of Lucky Strikes. Then I went down to the lake with my cousins and the next thing that happened was I was in the water.

I went down and down in the water.

I went down slowly. Even though the feeling of slowness was new to me, not part of my life, not the way I was, I was not scared. It was cool and silent and soft in the water and everything seemed to wave all around me, waving silently, and I kept my eyes open and I could look right up through the water and see the sun and almost see worlds far off and after a while the sun froze and everything in my mind froze.

And I thought, *I like this. I like this and this is the way it should be.* I heard a nice sound way far away and it was the slow-stretched sound of the steel guitar on the portable radio. I did not hear Hank Williams and The Drifting Cowboys, just the steel guitar.

I drowned, that's what everyone said. And when they took me

out of the lake, and I opened my eyes, and someone yelled, "Jesus saved her," and it was like everything in the world was just light and as perfect as it should be, so I thought maybe Jesus did save me, which is what a Savior would do.

I was not wild any longer. I was slow. I could feel the spaces in between deciding to do something, like waving hello, or blowing my nose, or turning on the radio, and my actually doing it. I could feel spaces when people said something to me and then I answered them. Or maybe I answered a question they had asked before, sometimes a long time before.

I liked being the way I was, the new way.

I grew up.

Tom came along. He was quite a pleasant man and strong. He had very long arms and fuzzy black eyebrows. He walked with a stoop and his long arms hanging. Once he told me when he was a boy other children used to call him "Monkey Boy." He said he used to make himself laugh at them and tell them they were wrong. He was no "Monkey Boy," he was *Mr. Monkey*, and then he'd make this sound like he was a man and an ape.

This is what Tom said to me: "You used to be a nervous girl. But now you're not nervous. You're all peaceful. Sometimes you're so peaceful that people do not take the least notice of you."

"Oh," I said.

"I notice you," Tom said.

Maybe it was sometime later, he asked, "Are you lonely?"

"I don't know," I said.

"I think you are lonely," Tom said.

"All right."

"What if I marry you?" Tom said. "How would that be? You wouldn't be lonely then." Then he smiled. "Mr. Monkey won't be lonely either. Maybe you can teach Mr. Monkey how to be peaceful."

Well, I did marry him. We had Alice and then Johnny and then Carla.

What happened next was Tom went away to be a soldier.

Then he came back.

He was different. He said he had to cry sometimes. He said he had too many bad pictures always running in his head. He said he wanted to really be a monkey and not a person because people did terrible things to each other, just terrible things, and he said he needed me to hold him and bring him peacefulness and I did.

Then Tom died. One day, when he woke up, he started to cough. He said he was not worried. He said nobody ever died of a cough. But he did die of a cough, you could say, but it wasn't on the day the cough started. It was later.

After Tom died, I got a job at Bell and Howell as "projector tester." (*Projector Tester* are words you can say over and over in your mind, aren't they, like a sweet lullaby about colors or something that tastes very good. They are slow words. I think they may be words that come from outer space.)

Projector Tester is a good job. You have to give new Bell and Howell projectors a three minute test. If you turn them on and the bulb doesn't pop right away and you can show your film all the way through, then the Quality Control department will certify the projection lamp for a year. If a bulb is going to go, it goes quick: POP! That is how people should die, I think, only not with the POP!

So here is what I do. I line up twelve just manufactured 8mm projectors on the test table. Then I plug them in to the twelve-outlet silver metal electrical strip. Next I click a little reel of film on the upper spindle of each machine. It's the three-inch reel with fifty feet of film. On our newest model, the top-of-the-line Bell and Howell 8mm Lumina, the threading of the film is fully automatic and you never have to touch the film or the filmgate. You put the film's leader here and *zip-click-clich*, the film is automatically threaded!

The 8mm Bell and Howell Lumina also features a retractable power cord and full auto- focus. It is quite a good movie projector.

The test movies are all samples from Castle Films, Inc. (I am sorry, you will not get a sample film with the purchase of the 8mm Bell and Howell Lumina projector. If you wish to purchase Castle films, they are sold at camera stores or may be ordered from the Castle Film Catalog.)

Castle films run three minutes each. I like that. In three minutes, you get the whole story. Some Castle films are in color, cartoons like Woody Woodpecker in *Fowled Up Falcon* or travel films like *Hawaii: Enchanted Isle* (#9138), and some are in black and white, like the Abbot and Costello films (these are very funny three-minute movies and I think I would laugh very hard at them but when I start to laugh, why, I sometimes think Lou Costello reminds me of someone and I get to thinking about who and so I don't laugh after all), and *Chimp's Last Chance* (#855). There are many Castle films about chimps and apes and gorillas: I think it was Tom who told me that chimps and apes and gorillas are not the same except for apes and gorillas.

There is one three-minute Castle film called *Mysterious Dr. Satan*. In it, the hero is the Copperhead and he wears a mask and fights a robot. It was so interesting I even told Johnny about it but I do not think he understood.

When I click the master switch all the projectors show all the movies together on the wall (except for the 8mm Lumina projection lamps that go POP) and Abbot and Costello meet Chilly Willy and there's the chimps and Coney Island and The Three Little Bruins and Audie Murphy and W C Fields and a robot and Lon Chaney the Man-Made monster. It's like a stew of movies on the wall.

Projectors with popped bulbs I put on the FAILED shelf and the rest I pack up and put on the three-tiered cart.

That is what my job is, and now that you know, why, you see why I felt bad I had to take half a day off when the school called about Johnny.

This time it was not just a note home. Mother Cordelia said the school needed to talk to me and that meant she needed to talk to me.

So on Tuesday, I put on my hat and gloves and went to school. Christ the Comforter is a very good school with statues and pictures and flags. Mother Cordelia is principal. When she talks to me, she turns her head in a way that makes me think she will just keep turning it and turning it and it will go around and around and around. "Johnny runs up to the other students and blasts them in the face with bubbles." Mother Cordelia laughs but I don't because Mother Cordelia doesn't look like anything is funny. Laughing is not always about funny. "I guess you could say he's forever blowing bubbles," Mother Cordelia says, "but he's shooting them from that toy, that ray gun."

"Oh," I say. "Well. Then. Yes." That is the kind of thing I say when I need to put words out there but cannot be certain of what to say. It is strange, almost like being underwater, or getting secret messages from outer space, but just then, I can see in my mind Chilly Willy and gorillas and bubbles of light going pop-pop-POP!

Mother Cordelia says when Johnny "blows bubbles at the other children, he yells he is CAPTAIN RAMJET of THE ROCKET REBELS and he will destroy them all with his bubbles of death. We do not like children to make this sort of threat, even playfully. And, frankly, I do not think Johnny is being all that playful."

I tell Mother Cordelia Johnny has no father.

"But Johnny has a Father." She points to the Crucifix on the wall by the window. She says, "Johnny's Eternal Father is always with him. Our Father who art in heaven."

I nod my head. *Woody Woodpecker. Mighty Mouse. Fatso Bear. Chimp on the Farm.*

"It's the comic books," Mother Cordelia tells me. "Johnny is obsessed by comic books."

These are Johnny's comic books: OUTER SPACE INVADERS. BEYOND THE GALAXY. DARK DIMENSION 12X. SPACE MONSTERS. BUZZ COREY. ATOMIC MENACE. CAPTAIN RAMJET OF THE ROCKET REBELS. ROGUE STAR. FLASH GORDON. PIRATES OF THE STRATOSPHERE. ROD BROWN OF THE ROCKET RANGERS.

"You must take the comics away from him," Mother Cordelia says. "Get him away from the comic books."

"All right," I tell her.

"No more comic books," Mother Cordelia says, "because you know what is good for him and right."

"Yes," I say. *Chilly Willy is so silly and now the Mt. Everest Woodpeckers return on the Gorilla Show ...*

"I further advise," says Mother Cordelia, "that you have a serious talk with him and then give him ... You. Know. What."

"All right," I say.

"And I advise still further that you give it to him right on his ... You. Know. Where."

Now Mother Cordelia smiles.

"All right," I say.

"I am sure ... You. Know. How." Now Mother Cordelia winks.

I know what is right and good for my children. That evening, I tell Johnny and Carla that Alice I am taking them on a picnic.

I like picnics.

III

Ro-man set up headquarters and base of operations in a cave in the Valley of Bad Shaped Rocks. (Coincidentally, this was the exact cave site where Johnny and Carla had come upon The

Professor and Roy practicing archaeology.) Though he was but a lone warrior, and a hairy one at that, Ro-man had been ordered to destroy all of humanity.

Check and double check, Ro was up for the gig. Ro-man was equipped with a Calcinator ray, a bubble machine, a Televisory Vidscreen and a card table. Wouldn't take much more than that. This was before the Star Wars missile defense system.

No declaration of intent, no cheeseball speeches like THE DAY THE EARTH STOOD STILL. Ro-man royally Japs the planet. Fired up the old Calcinator ray and, brother, that's all she wrote.

Reports via viewscreen that he has put the kibosh on the whole kit 'n' kaboodle. It's a wrap. Case closed, Mabel, and I'm coming home.

That's what Ro-man brags to The Great Guidance, who more or less tells Ro-man, "*Bubbe*, you are so full of prunes." Cram this into your noggin, Ro-man, there are SIX PEOPLE still alive on the planet so let's get calcinating."

Little did Ro-man know that Johnny had been spying, picking up on the two-way interplanetary gas session and bombast between the Great Guidance and Ro-man.

Johnny beat feet back to the ruined house: all that was left was the basement level. Strands of wire buzzing and crackling with electricity—a primitive but effective means of blocking Ro-man's Televisory Probes—surrounded the open air bunker of the last human beings on the plant, who were—

Pop: (who *had been* The Professor but ... Hey, change happens) and

Mom: (ding-dong ding-dong)

and

Carla (ain't she sweet?)

and

Roy, who was now the scientist boy-friend

of

Alice, who had become a scientist in her own right.

And of course ... Here's Johnny!

Johnny threw himself into the sanctuary and says, "I know where Ro-man is. Let's go and kill him."

Alice: Perhaps we *could* find his weak spot.

Mom: Do you think it will rain today? It could. I wish we had a roof. I don't think we have an umbrella and we are not fish.

Roy: Maybe ... his *ass*. We could jam some fissionable materials right up Ro-man's old wazoo ...

Pop: Don't talk like that.

Alice: Roy, your levity is inappropriate. We are confronting certain death.

Roy: Oh ... Alice, will you marry me?

Carla: I thought you were already playing house.

Mom and Pop: Ha-ha.

It was agreed then. Alice and Roy, having in common both science and a penchant for kludgy banter, would wed.

Roy: ... we were wondering how you'd feel about performing the ceremony.

Pop/Professor: You want me to—?

Alice: Oh, yes!

Professor: In that case, let's do it! And I want you to know this is the biggest social event of the year! The whole darn town will turn out!

Pop/Professor is really a big tickle. Har-de-har-har. But okay, if Jackie Leonard he ain't, leave us not to forget he was the cat who, with the invaluable aid of scientists Roy and his own daughter Alice, invented an ANTIBIOTIC SERUM capable of curing all diseases, even the common cold.

And upon whom did he experiment with the first injections? Turn around, drop your pants, and a little *shtoch in tuchus* for his family and Roy and of course, Himself.

Interesting side effect, one which The Professor had no time to learn from FDA trials. *The antibiotic also provided complete immunization to Ro-man's death ray!*

Which fact gets glommed onto by ... Ro-man.

Ro-Man: Great Guidance, I have discovered the secret of our failure to destroy the remaining humans! Our Calcinator death ray cannot penetrate them. They have been made immune through the antibiotic serum, which I believe is the same as our formula X-Z-A.

The Great Guidance had new commands.

Ro-Man: I am ordered to kill the humans. I must do it with my hands.

Professor: Dearly beloved, we are gathered here to ... Dear Lord, You know I am not trained for this job. But I have tried to live by your laws. The Ten Commandments ... The beatitudes ... The Golden Rule.

I have always believed in the Brotherhood of Man. I have always believed that one day, the working peoples of the world would unite to throw off the yoke of Oppression. The working class is the class that works and thus, we, the last survivors, reach out to any other last survivors who might have survived in Russia.

(When you're a Red, you're a Red until you're dead.)

Professor: Father on high, I would like you to give your blessing to Alice and Roy. Even in this darkest hour, we have kept the faith. In your grand design, there may be no room for man's triumph over this particular evil that has beset us. If, by any chance, we workers of the world emerge in strength and victory should be on our side, I want You to give a long life to Alice and Roy, and a fruitful one. But no matter how it ends, Lord, watch over them this night ... Watch over us all.

Amen.

And now, I pronounce you Man and Wife.

Roy, do you have the ring?

Roy: Why, I didn't think about that.

Johnny said, "Oh, brother." Johnny thought, *Stupid a-hole. Freame supreme. And he's a swish.*

Mom took off her own ring and handed it to Roy. "Rings go around and around," she said.

Roy: With this ring, I thee wed.

Professor: The only thing to seal it now is a kiss.

They kissed. Johnny asked, "Where are you going on your honeymoon, Niagara Falls?"

Roy (laughing): Lad, you are just chockful of scintillating wit. To tell the truth, we hadn't thought about that.

Professor: Wherever you go—be careful. And I want you back first thing in the morning. After all, there is a war going on! And now, more than ever, I don't want to give up!

Roy: Thanks for everything, Dad. Most of all, for having raised Alice. You too, Mom.

Alice: I'll go get my things, and then we'll go.

ALICE

And so, high-ho and off I go, a'hand in hand, a'honeymooning with Roy, lah-de-dah, Roy, dunce-in-residence. "Alice," says he, "we really need to talk." A pause, then, "I need to talk."

I'd wager a dollar to your Aunt Nellie's discount diaphragm that Roy is struggling with a confession concerning the "love that dare not speak its name"—or even lisp it.

But why should I make it easy? "No, my dear, my darling, my one and only tutti-frutti. What we need is FORNICATION. The future of the human race depends on it. As soon as we find a little out of the way nook or cranny, you're going to jam your beef bayonet into my yummy gummy and ride me like a carnival tilt-a-whirl. We are fucking for the future, Roy, a better bet than US Savings Bonds."

A sidelong glance shows me red-face Roy about to have a cow.

Do the dirty with Roy? Please, My Ain True Love is a Magnificence of Savagery and Intellect. He is Unpredictability and Contrasts. He is Cruelty and Confused Gentleness. Fate has brought him to me and me to him. He's one hotcha-hotcha and I'm totally gone for him. As Blaise Pascal said, "The heart has its reasons which reason knows not of." And as Dale Evans stated, "Every time we love, every time we give, it's Christmas."

So, Merry Christmas to me, as we continue on, Roy trying to talk and me following my unreasoning heart.

Then behind us, Carla calls out. "Roy, Alice, wait for me!" And we stop, turn, and here she comes, cutie-pie in Keds.

Alice: Carla, what are you doing here?

"I didn't get you any presents," Carla says with reach-for-the-insulin adorability, holding out a droopy flower.

"How lovely," Roy says sourly, perhaps thinking of his own pointdexter, likely to droop when summoned to report for duty.

Carla's following us was unexpected, all right, but perhaps it is better this way, I think, as I gush appropriately. "Oh, you little rascal! Thank you very much. Now, you'd better run right on

home!"
Roy: Quickly, Carla.
Very good, fly away home, little birdbrain, fly away home.

───

She runs and runs, puffs of dust trailing her. She is afraid now and she tries to think of things that will make her not afraid. Maybe Johnny will play house with her. Maybe Mom will sing her a song: "Chilly Willy cooked in a stew, with a penguin and a monkey and a girl like you." Of course, maybe she will be in bad trouble. Maybe Dad will be mad and yell and spank. Then for no reason she thinks, Maybe this is all a dream. Maybe she is drowning—little girls do drown—and in her drowning she is imagining this.

Suddenly, Ro-man blocks her path. Beneath his dull gray helmet, he has a broad and thick body like the hairiest of apes, although he stands easily erect, not even a hint that he'd feel more comfortable with knuckles on the ground. He looks like his feet hurt badly and you can tell he doesn't want to run because he is more the lumbering than the running type. Ro-man's face (what you can see of it through the misty none-too-clean glass visor of his helmet) is something like Lon Chaney's in *Phantom of the Opera*, if in addition to his other physiognomic misfortunes, the Phantom had been badly burned in a fire, or had decided to don two silk stockings to rob a currency exchange. Ro-man's space helmet sports one bent antenna and one straight one.

Reception is pretty good, considering.
Ro-Man: What are you doing here alone, girl-child?
Carla (sans cuteness): My daddy won't let you hurt me.
Ro-Man: We will see!

It seems she was right to be afraid. She is neither drowning nor dreaming and she is in bad, bad trouble.

───

Ro-man contacts the Great Guidance on the Televisory Vidscreen. Ro-man's got plans. Ro-man's got dreams. Ro-man's gotta be cool and just mayhap, Mr. Ro-man, Esq. might have it made in the shade.

Ro-Man: Great Guidance, I have a favorable report. I have already eliminated one of them. It was a simple matter of ... strangulation. That leaves four for me to kill.

The Great Guidance: Error again! *Five.*

You can hear the Great Guidance's exasperation: *What's with you, Schmuck? You're coming on like Goof Majorus. You a numbnuts or what?*

Ro-Man: *Four,* well ... I have made an estimate in relation to our strategic reserve: The plan should include ONE LIVING HUMAN for reference, in case of unforeseen contingency.

The Great Guidance: Do you question the plan?

Ro-Man: No, Great One. I only postulate—

The Great Guidance implies, *Hold on just one chicken-pluckin' second! Oh, Ro-man, I'm tuning in and the picture is clear! You've gone APE for the female HUMAN, the one with the classy chassis and the outsized nay-nays. 'Fess up, you got a case of the trottin' hots for the babe.*

Ro-Man: I ...

Great Guidance: Proceed on schedule! Destroy the others. ALL OF THEM!

Ro-Man cuts the Vidscreen.

Ro-Man (goes all existential à la Hamlet's "to be or not to be," only with more hair and a space helmet: I cannot, and yet I must. How do you calculate that? At what point on the graph do *must* and *cannot* meet? Yet, I must.

But I cannot.

ALICE

Believe it or not, despite the rock-strewn terrain, we found a small patch of grass, spread out the blanket, and then, just for the hell of it, I surprised Roy with a sudden and fierce kiss.

He did not surprise me in the least. He pulled back, wiping his lips with the back of his hand. "Alice ..."

I said, "Our obligation to the future generation is to create it, so let's get propagating."

"Yessss," Roy said super-sibilantly. "I take our responsibility seriously, but it will be difficult, because my natural inclinations ..."

"You're light in the shoes? You're a bigger fairy than Tinker

113

Belle? You really love FRUIT cake and NANCY comics and JUDY GARLAND, too? Aw, you nutty nob jockey, you flying flit, you silly shirtlifter, you fucky-sucky Stoke on Trent, I knew you were a ragin' HOMO ever since I first saw you. There's as much chance of my making humpity-bumpers with you as there is my diddling Dwight D. Eisenhower in the window at Macy's during the Thanksgiving Day parade while Mamie farts "Auld Lang Syne" in three quarter time."

Color Roy confused. "You don't love me?"

I smiled.

Enter ... *RO-MAN!*

Enter ... My Own True Love!

... who gave Roy such a _zetz_ that stars orbited his head like in a Woody Woodpecker cartoon. Ro-man said something along the lines of "Alice and I are going steady, pal, so you're cruisin' for a bruisin'."

Ro-man, my Romantic Ro-man!

So that's all she wrote, Roy. Off to the Great Fruit Stand in the Sky. As William Shakespeare had it, "Nothing in his life became him like the leaving it."

"C'mon, Big Guy," I said, and Ro-man picked me up in his great, long arms, My Big Loving Monkey Man, and held me tight against his powerful hairiness as he carried me off to our cave.

It was easy to lure Mom, Pop, and the Obnox to the cave. Hello, Operator, get me the Televisory Vidscreen of the last remaining Humans on Earth. Ooh, ooh, Mommy, Poppy, the Big Bad Hairy Guy in the Helmet has your poor widdle Alice and I only just managed to get to this communicator while he's recalibrating and recalculating his recalcinator. You've got to rescue me.

And here they come. Mom going woo-woo, Pop singing "The Internationale"—and the Obnox. *(You tell me your dream/I'll tell you mine.)*

And when they're at the mouth of the cave, Ro-man clunks Mom and Pop's heads together KA-THUNK! (*Nyuck-nyuck-nyuck, you hapless halfwits!)* Ro-man grabs Snotty Johnny by the googler and sets to squeezing.

Takes maybe five seconds, all in all. The three of them lie

there, as dead as Adlai (Commie Symp) Stevenson's presidential plans.

And now, I, I and my Strange and Wondrous Love, can begin, Adam and Eve, on this world that is ours and ours alone ...

THE GREAT GUIDANCE: You wish to be a human? Good, you can die a human!
The Great Guidance gestures. Lighting shoots from his fingers.
Zap!
Ro-man staggers and falls dead. Nonplussed, Alice says, "Shit."

ROBOT MONSTER, DREAMING

Though in many aspects the Anthropoid Ape resembles the Lowland and Mountain Gorillas of Africa, there are marked differences originally noted and recorded by enlightened zoologists of the mid-19th century. The true Anthropoid weighs less than and is not as stocky as his evolutionary underling, the Gorilla. An Anthropoid walks fully erect with no knuckle-dragging and considerably more grace and poise, has a rudimentary but practical language consisting mainly of noun and verbs, and by any measurable scale, is of far greater intelligence than your maggot-eating, shit-flinging ape.

Which is to say that in their natural habitat and conditions, gorillas are fucking morons and Anthropoid Apes are merely pitifully stupid. If this sounds judgmental, ah, mine is the right: It was my curse to be born Anthropoid. Indeed, from my entrance onto this Earthly plane, was I doubly cursed: Though all was proper for an anthropoid infant from my neck down, I was born with the face of a wrinkled, double-ugly infant human being.

Speculate as you will, and certainly as I often did, there is a simplistic legend among Anthropoids. Yes, now I know about Archetypes and Collective Unconscious and all that, but trust me; with your typical Anthropoid having at best a low double-digit IQ, we are talking about a *super-simplistic* mythology:

Once, long ago, an orphan infant human boy was adopted into a tribe of Anthropoids and grew up to be *Tarmangani*. The Great

White Ape. He learned from his extended foster family how to sleep safely in trees and flee the claws and fangs of Numa, the Lion, and to keep from being trampled by Tantor when the seasonal mating-madness came upon the tusked behemoth. On his own, he learned the use of a knife (my unimaginative clansmen refer to it as a "hand fang") to read and write English, French, German and Spanish, and, for all I know, how to floss three times a day, use a Zippo lighter, and strum "Whispering" on the tenor banjo.

With smarts like that, Tarmangani soon established himself as King of the Apes. I would assume he suffered an epiphany one day: *I am* Ruler *of this bunch of hairy, stinky shitheads? I am dying for good conversation, for a seven course meal that includes no fruits, leaves, shoots, or grubs, for a dance with a non-hirsute someone of the opposite sex who can waltz or polka rather than stomp around grunting and farting at the ceremonial Dum-Dum.* Intellectually, Tar had gone far above his raising, and so can it be any surprise that he abandoned those who'd taken him in and given him food, shelter, and, on occasion, a backhanded smack to the chops?

It is whispered that Tarmangani will return one day. Myself, I don't care if he does return in glory, riding a white ass though the jungle, while all the assholic anthropoids wave palm leaves and chant, "*Ben Gund Yud* (The Great Leader returns)! Hosanna in the highest! Now there'll be fat larvae in every pot! Huzzah, huzzah, huzzah!" Frankly, once my own brain cells were energized and making connections, putting two plus two together and working quadratic equations on the side, I couldn't buy it: Tarmangani would never come back to this. I sure as hell would not. Not while Howard Johnson's offers thirty-one flavors.

I mention the legend only as it's thinly conceivable that it supplies a clue as to how I came by my countenance. Genetically, anthropoids and humans are 99+% the same. It is not impossible, methinks thinks me, that Great White Ape grew tired of playing pat his own cake and held his nose long enough to plant his Tarmanganiness into an Anthropoid lass, maybe he got drunk, and then, recessive and dominant genes at work ...

Ah, why am I here? Why was I born? What the fuck? Such philosophical questions can and will be contemplated even unto the End Times—and if you come up with the definitive answer,

I'll see you get your shot on The 64 Dollar Question.

I know only that I grew up with an ugly human face on top of my neck. Other little anthropoids called me "*Balu Ug Lot,*" which translates "Little Baby Ass Face," and my own mother, Gloopit by name, used to wrinkle up her nose, nostrils as big as Oldsmobile headlights, and grunt most un-mommyish phrases.

I was outcast and exile. Oh, I maintained contact with my peers and their elders—my ass was frequently contacted by a foot of a playmate, my head, a fist—but I was the classic ugly duckling, the lonely little petunia in the onion patch, the matzo ball in the Irish stew.

Until one day ... Fate intervened.

Fate! There is no fate. Between the thought and the success God is the only agent. Do you know who proclaimed that? Edward G. Bulwer-Lytton, who created some of the worst prose in the English language, perhaps outdone only by his friend and crashing snob and bore Charles Dickens.

I can give you a thousand quotations, pertinent or impertinent. I can build a harpsichord and admirably perform upon it no fewer than 300 Bach cantatas despite my having fingers like Polish sausage. If you need someone to offer critical thought on cave wall painters or Caillebotte, cite each season's batting average for Monte Stratton, or espouse a credible opinion on why Cyril and Methodius should not be credited with devising the Glagolitic alphabet, good sir, I am your huckleberry!

And how did this happen?

Why, one day in the skies overhead there was an eye-searing flash and eardrum-shattering explosion. And then, no more than a kilometer from us, an earth shaking impact.

"*Pandar pandar!*" yelled one—"my people."

"*Zu tu!*" shouted another.

And of course, the obvious "*Kreeg Kreeg-gah!*"

"Loud, loud!" and "Big Bright!" and "Beware, danger, danger!" Such were the keen observations of my landsmen.

Please remember, I had not yet metamorphosed into the Einstein of the Anthropoids, but there was a brute force of curiosity within me that overcame my fear.

What had I to lose? My life? As Cesare Pavese has it: "No one ever lacks a good reason for suicide." Human or Anthropoid, both species have an occasional and enviable bent for self- destruction.

117

Or perhaps I was yet too fucking stupid to know there might be danger involved.

With the cheerful encouragement of the tribe, "Numa will eat you if he can shut his eyes so he doesn't have to look at you," and "*Ngh amba wob at!*" (Don't trip over your little bitty penis), I set off.

I found the wreckage of a flying saucer. (I of course did not know then it was any such thing.) I discovered a grayish dead body, non-anthropoid and non-*zan-mangani.* If you are in the *Mangani* family, you normally have five digits per hand. This little *pisher* had three. He also had big glassy eyes like some of the bugs I used to find pretty tasty.

And I found ... I did not know what it was, not then, but it was round and gray and like any babbling human toddler or most primitive mammals equipped with hands / paws, I had to try it on.

My head lights up like Coney Island. It is like I'm getting the extra A-Bomb they'd planned to drop on Tokyo if Hiroshima and Nagasaki didn't do the trick.

Epistemological Instant! "What is knowledge?" "How do we know what we know?" "How is knowledge acquired?"

You don't have to send in to the Rosicrucians, *amigo.* I can testify and proclaim without contradiction knowledge is acquired Just! Like! That! *Zappo-Bam! Bang! Pow! Zoom!* Maybe not the sum total of all Earthly knowledge and that of the worlds beyond, but a damned good bunch for a freeby was contained in the helmet I lowered down over my "accursed ugliness" (that's a literary allusion, *bwah*: Gaston Leroux's *Phantom of the Opera*). I could untangle Tesla and find the Lost Chord, mesmerize the masses and perfect perpetual motion, and even proffer a kōan spun off from the last words of Dutch Schultz: "A boy has never wept nor dashed a thousand kim."

"You mean, 'The boy has wept and also dashed a thousand kim?' Then the wet bird does indeed fly at night."

Thus I became the intelligent anthropoid with the ugly human face.

I fear to remove the helmet. I do not think it would happen, but it is just possible I could revert to my pre-smart state. I could not bear that, to descend to once more being an obtuse pariah.

Because, while I am ever so solitary now, the only one of my kind upon this planet (*uberanthropoid!*), I dare to hope there are other beings—human beings—who may come to look upon me and discern only my mind ...

And if there is such a thing (the helmet does not impart any knowledge of the matter!) my SOUL!

O Joseph Carey Merrick, O Elephant Man, You of Hideous Visage and Victim of a Thousand upon a Thousand Torments, did you not at last find Kindness, did you not come to know Compassion, and to possess companions with whom you might laugh and weep and speak of the Pyramids and poetry and cabbages and kings and all things great and small?

I set forth upon my quest, and Joseph Carey Merrick, you are Inspiration and Companion.

Courage, Friend Merrick whispers, and I take courage, and *Hope*, Friend Merrick whispers, and I take hope
that
my loneliness might reach out
to touch the lonely
those who carry their own sad and frozen
exile within themselves
that
we will meet
The Lonely
that
we will come to know one another that
we will love
that
we will love
that
we will love

PRAYER

The man floats to seeming awareness, though dazed, then descends once more into unconsciousness. His dry lips sometimes make a tiny _peh-peh_ noise, like something you'd hear in the woods late at night without recognizing the source.

Then he says quite plainly, "Tylenol."

They surround you with comfort. Angels.
No, those who will help you die.
Are you in pain?
Should I get you something?
Do you need something, Mr. Jablonski? Hank?
It's all right. You think you've said that but you can't be sure.
You open your eyes.
The priest is here. Nice guy. You've spoken with him.
Filipino, hardly any accent.
He's here to give you Last Rites.
He's here for your confession.

April 16, 2015
Unit 17
Hospice of the Comforter

The airy sunlight suffuses the room.
The Christ on the crucifix above the bed seems at peace.
Hank. That's what he asked to be called when the Comforter took him in. Hank, Henry Jablonski.
A good man, a good Catholic.
Hank Jablonski had sense, knew that he would most likely be alone for this—transition— and so he planned wisely and the

money saved by years of frugality would take care of his earthly ending and what was left over would go to the church.

The chaplain of the Comforter, Father Witmer Tortosa, seated at the bedside, has talked with Father Kelso at St. Joseph the Worker, and knows the regard Hank's parish priest has for this dying man. Hank was working class, bought a house on the GI Bill, married young: Laura, his high school sweetheart. Maybe the last generation to do all right without a college degree: Sold janitorial supplies and washroom cleaning services. Lost his wife to cancer when their only child was eight.

Mary was the daughter's name.

Sad about Mary, tragic, but Hank accepted the will of God.

Hank Jablonski had faith.

Hank's eyes are closed, his face placid, but his lips move.

Father Witmer Tortosa leans in closer. Hank's breath is sweet, like flowers.

"Mr. ... Hank?" Though he does not call Hank "my son"—the thirty-three-year-old Father Witmer was ordained only two years ago—he feels the eternal connection of Holy Mother Church, that blessed assurance, that he and this man share.

They believe.

In an age of unbelief and disbelief and disdain of belief, they believe.

They believe in the Father and the Son and the Holy Spirit.

They believe in salvation.

They believe in prayer.

Yes, Father Witmer has sometimes doubted his own personal abilities, sometimes questioned not what God has asked of him, never that, but his own adequacy when he has been summoned to do what a priest must, to ease the fears of the dying, to help them leave this world in a state of grace so that they might dwell forever with the Lord.

But Father Witmer does not doubt: *Blessed be the name of the Lord.*

"Hank?" Father Witmer touches Hank Jablonski's shoulder, not expecting an answer, lucidity.

"Father Witmer." Hank's voice is quiet but does not seem

weak or even for that matter old.

"I am here," Father Witmer says.

"There were four Marys," Hank says. "I don't believe that was coincidence. Oh, I didn't understand it then and do not fully understand it now. My daughter was Mary. There were other Marys ..."

6:30 A.M.
Wednesday September 29, 1982
Elk Grove Village, Illinois

She wakes with a scratchy throat and a sniffily nose. She does not want to stay home from school. She likes school.

Her mom talks sense. She needed to stay home today, really, so she can nip this in the bud and besides, she doesn't want to infect others.

You're not being a friend when you share your viruses, her father says. Stay in your pajamas, kiddo, watch some *Love Boat* reruns. Drink lots of OJ. Take a Tylenol.

And she reluctantly says okay and next thing you know, there's a heavy thump and her father finds her unconscious on the bathroom floor.

The paramedics are damned good. If there had been a way to save her, they'd have saved her.

She is pronounced dead at Alexian Brothers Medical Center in Elk Grove Village.

She was twelve years old.

Her name was Mary.

April 16, 2015
Unit 17
Hospice of the Comforter

"Your daughter? I do not understand."

Is that a ticking laugh or a faint precursor of the death gurgle? It is not a sound that Father Witmer has ever before heard. Its unfamiliarity disturbs him like a subtle threat.

"No, you do not understand."

⌒━⌒

Eight people dead.
Eight people dead.
How many times during how many sleepless nights
did you tell yourself you were not responsible. You
had to say it aloud sometimes, like a prayer, like
saying the Rosary:
I did not kill them.
I did not kill them.
But the one, that one ...
Evil. He was truly evil.
But even so, I did not kill him.
I did not.
God killed him.

Father Witmer says, "The dead people."
Hank has been whispering: *Marys and dead people and terrible nights without sleep. A God Who killed ...*
The word most clearly enunciated: Evil.
Father Witmer senses this is not the incoherent muttering of a man giving up the ghost. Father Witmer cannot stop himself from thinking he is on the verge of learning something dreadful and important.
Like working a toothache that you probe to greater pain with the tip of your tongue, Father Witmer urges, "Tell me."

Mary Jablonski grew up motherless and step-motherless.
You see, things were different back then. I lost my Laura, lost her when I loved her so much. That was it. I knew there would never be another woman for me.
Mary had the nuns at St. Joseph's, and they were good to her, they were very kind and patient, and across the street, we had the Lawsons and the Radeckis, and they had lots of kids, lots of girls, and she was with them all the time. Right after school, she'd go right over to Toni and Louise Radecki's house and be there until I got home from work, and if I was going to be late, I'd call and Mrs. Radecki would feed her. Oh, we lived in the suburbs and

people were laughing even back then about how the suburbs are dull and how everyone in each ticky-tacky house was really all alone, but that's not how it was: we had neighborhoods with good people and it was okay.

Mary never gave me one bit of trouble. Never. I'm being truthful, not just because I loved her and was so proud of her and not just because I lost her. I remember, she wanted a hamster when she was in third grade. The deal was, it would be *her* hamster and she had to take care of it. So she got the hamster— she called it Snorky, like that TV show, *The Banana Splits*—and she took care of it. I never had to do a thing, not even remind her. And when Snorky died, we talked

about it, I remember, and then we buried her hamster. She never wanted another pet, not even a fish.

The closest Catholic high school was twenty-two miles away. It was the other direction from my territory so taking her and picking her up, well, it just wouldn't have been practical ...

Okay, tell the truth, I couldn't really afford it.

Lots of Catholic kids went to the public high school, Arlington Heights. It was fine. She liked it. She got good grades. She didn't do drugs or alcohol.

Seventeen, she wants to date and I talk with Mrs. Radecki about it and we set up rules and all. I meet the guys she dates, and they're okay high school guys, a couple with hair longer than I care for, but it's okay, they're nice enough, and really, there was never anything serious going on, not then.

And I felt God was watching over her, my Mary.

I don't understand the ways of God. We see through a glass darkly, but there will be a time when we will understand. I've talked a lot about this with Father Brennan and then Father Kelso when he replaced Father Brennan.

We know God is there and watches over us ... I believe that.

So Mary graduates and takes courses at Moser Secretarial School in Chicago, she rides in on the train, and no surprise, she graduates with honors and gets a good job at Sears. She's living at home, saving money, thinking about buying a clean used Pacer—yeah, people bought Pacers back then, funny looking cars—and then she meets him.

I liked him. I liked the way he smiled, like he wasn't too full of himself, and I liked his handshake, because it didn't say he had anything to prove, and I liked the way he treated Mary, always the gentleman.

I liked him.

I *liked* him.

He told me, after they'd been dating for a while, that way back when the boat got to the USA, great grandpa realized if you want to succeed in this country, it's better for your name not to have too many "Cs" or "Zs" or end in an "i" or an "o."

That's how Kwiatkowski became Kwiat.

That was his name: John Kwiat.

⎯ ⎯⎯

"So many," Hank says. His eyes open. He looks at the priest and Father Witmer can feel himself being seen.

"Can you tell me why so many had to die, Father?"

Noon
Wednesday September 29, 1982

The second person to be killed was Adam Janus. He was twenty-seven years old, had a civil service job, the PO, but stayed home that day. Not feeling well. The sniffles.

Had some lunch.

Going to take two Tylenol and get some rest.

A few minutes later, staggers into the kitchen and collapses.

Taken to Northwest Community Hospital.

Pronounced dead.

3:45 P.M.
September 29, 1982
Winfield, Illinois

They call her Lynn, Lynn Reiner.

She is twenty-seven.

There's a new baby at home, the Reiners' fourth child.

An excellent mother, her husband later said.

Not feeling well, general achiness.

Two Extra-Strength Tylenol.

She is pronounced dead at Central DuPage Hospital.

125

Lynn Reiner.
Her full name: Mary "Lynn" Reiner.

April 16, 2015
Unit 17
Hospice of the Comforter

"That was the third Mary."

"Yes," Father Witmer replies, as though having a rational conversation.

Silently, he prays:

> *Come, Holy Spirit,*
> *Replace the turbulence within us*
> *with a sacred calm.*
> *Replace the anxiety within us*
> *with a quiet confidence.*
> *Replace the fear within us*
> *with a strong faith.*

"The first Mary was my child."

Father, Son, Holy Spirit, Father Witmer prays. There seems a humid pressure around his head, a circling echo: *Marys and dead people and a God Who killed and Evil Evil Evil ...*

⸺⸺⸺

She came home late from a date with John Kwiat, much later than usual. I was in bed, pretty much asleep, just enough to hear her bedroom door close maybe louder than normal— maybe.

Next day, Saturday, I'm up at maybe 8:30 but Mary's not around. That's not like her. She's the original early bird.

I knock on her door.

Go away, is what she says, and she doesn't sound right.

No, let's talk, Mary.

No, go away.

The door's locked. I rattle the handle.

Mary.

And I wait a while and the door opens and there she is, and

she isn't in a nightgown—still wearing her Friday night clothes—and she has been crying, and she looks bad.

Daddy ...

Tell me.

And I try to put my arms around her but she doesn't let me. She backs up and then we're both sitting side by side on her rumpled-up but still-made bed.

Please, I say to her, please talk to me.

And after what seems like a long time, she does. She tells me and it sounds like she's reading a foreign language. She can make out the words, but not their meaning.

And I am praying, Jesus, Jesus, Jesus, but not aloud, and when I take her hand, she doesn't pull away.

We can't let him ...

Maybe it was my fault. Maybe I encouraged him. I don't know. He started, when he started, I should have said No, and then ... I don't know.

But he had no right ...

Jesus, Jesus, Jesus.

I want to kill him.

You can't do anything. You can't. You know what would happen to you. I don't know what would happen to me.

The police.

No! I'm ashamed. I am ashamed. No one can know! No one can ever know.

Will you pray with me?

She does. At least she gets down on her knees with me. And I am praying and maybe she is praying but her prayers end with sobbing.

I thought, or maybe I thought I thought, it would be okay.

Then one day I get home from work. The day had been fairly warm for autumn, right around 55-60, but it was kind of drizzly. A lot of days felt drizzly.

Mary was in the garage.

She was hanging from a few feet of clothesline.

Her face was so blue it was almost black.

That was Tuesday, September 29, 1981.

I prayed.
This was how I prayed:

Lord,
Give me strength ...
No, Lord! I do not ask for strength to bear my suffering.
All must suffer.
On the Cross, the Son of God suffered and died.
We *all* suffer as we must.
Lord, I do not ask for my soul to be filled with compassion.
I do not want compassion because it would make me able to forgive. I do not want to forgive.
Our Father Who Art in Heaven, Our Father Who Sees all Things Upon this Earth, Our Father Who is the God of Righteousness and Fairness and Truth: Give me Justice!
Give me Justice!
In the name of the Father and the Son and the Holy Spirit.
Amen.

5:00 P.M.
Wednesday, September 29, 1982
Arlington Heights, Illinois

Adam Janus's younger brother Stanley and his wife, Theresa, left the hospital where Adam had been pronounced dead. They had a funeral to plan. They went to Adam's nearby home.

Stanley's head was pounding. His back hurt. A slipped disc, maybe, something, but he suffered from chronic back pain.

His wife gave him two Tylenol. She might have made a funny-in-sad-times remark like, "These are supposed to bring relief and I could use some myself," and then she took two Tylenol as well.

Maybe Stanley heard that comment before he went down.

Maybe Theresa regretted saying it as she fell.

6:30 P.M.
Wednesday, September 29, 1982
Lombard, Illinois

Mary McFarland was thirty-one years old, employed at the Illinois Bell telephone store. She had a severe headache, went into the employees' back room, took several Tylenol, and collapsed.

Mary McFarland was not pronounced dead until 3:15 in the morning of the next day at Good Samaritan Hospital in Downers Grove.

———

The fourth Mary.

———

The lab reports came in relatively quickly for an era before the ubiquitous computer. Six people had died of cyanide poisoning. Each victim had ingested 100 to 1,000 times the amount of potassium cyanide needed to cause death. Basically, cyanide asphyxiates you from within. It inhibits red blood cells from utilizing oxygen. In high doses, it usually causes a quick, but not merciful, death.

The hunch of an Arlington Heights public health nurse, Helen Jensen—whose sensitive sense of smell detected the scent of almonds—and the research of Dr. Thomas Kim, Medical Director of Northwest Community Hospital's ICU, and the investigations of the Cook County Medical Examiner's Office, the Chicago Police Department, and various northwest suburban police departments led to the conclusion that bottles of Tylenol had been taken from the shelves of various supermarkets and drug stores over a period of several weeks by person or persons

unknown, that said person or persons added the cyanide to the capsules, then returned to the stores to place the bottles back on the shelves. Five bottles were initially and correctly linked to these initial victims' deaths. Three other tampered-with bottles were discovered.

There was panic. Not just in and around Chicago. Across the

nation.

Johnson & Johnson, manufacturers of Tylenol, issued warnings and a recall of all Tylenol products. The company halted Tylenol production and put an indefinite hiatus on advertising. Johnson & Johnson executives consulted with their ad agencies about the possibility of regaining public trust.

Legislators frantically discussed the need for rapid reform in the laws and regulations for the packaging of over-the-counter substances.

The FBI established a strong link to the Chicago Police Department, Illinois suburban police departments, and police departments throughout the country.

The hunt was on for The Tylenol Killer.

April 16, 2015
Unit 17
Hospice of the Comforter

"What is it ... What is it you *are* telling me?" Father Witmer says. "You must tell me, you must unburden yourself. What is it ... What did you do?"

Hank does not answer.

Friday, October 1, 1982
Chicago, Illinois

She was blonde, and one of the rare people who truly could be deemed vivacious. Paula Prince lived in Old Town, which was being gentrified and cleansed of hippies to make way for the ascendant Yuppies. She was a flight attendant for United, loved flying, traveling, meeting new people.

But she had a headache, wanted to shake it before she met her sister for dinner, and so she went to Walgreen's and bought a bottle of Tylenol.

Surveillance cameras were not yet everywhere, but Walgreen's did have a camera focused on the counter.

There exists a videotape of Paula Prince purchasing her own death.

My Mary died and then Mary and then Adam and then Lynn Mary and then Stanley and then Theresa and then Mary and then Paula and I did not understand why they had to die did not even have a clue and there is yet so much I do not know and may never know God Who is God Now and Forever understands

Saturday, October 2, 1982
Schaumburg, Illinois

John Kwiat awakens with a Dr. Doom tequila shots hangover, but, don't do the crime if you can't do the time, right?

A little water splashed on the face, a little cold water sloshed into a glass, two Tylenol from the bottle in the medicine cabinet into the palm and here we go ...

And maybe there's time to think Uh-oh or maybe think, Nah, what are the odds, no problem, but in seconds, the whirl of acute dizziness hits and he's gasping for air and his legs won't hold him and then he's on the floor and convulsing and dying.

He is not found until Tuesday, October 5.

"I asked God for justice. He gave me justice. The others ... I do not understand. John Kwiat was justice."

Father Witmer wants to yell and is careful not to. "Did you kill John Kwiat?"

Then he whispers, "Did you kill the others?"

Hank's eyes are shut. There's that awful sound of his lips: *Peh-peh* noise.

Father Witmer administers the Last Rites of the Holy Catholic Church.

Father Witmer does not begin his research until the evening of Tuesday, April 21, a day after the burial of Henry Jablonski in Queen of Angels. He must. He cannot simply accept not knowing.

There are too many intimations of evil.

In his room at Hospice of the Comforter, he takes to his HP laptop and Google.

1982. It was the year he was born.

(Does this have meaning, that it was the year, too, of the Tylenol Murders?)

Now, in 2015, the case remains open.

Father Witmer learns no one was ever charged for tampering with the bottles of Tylenol.

Father Witmer learns no one was ever charged with murder.

Father Witmer learns there were seven victims of the Tylenol Killer: Mary Kellerman, Adam Janus, Lynn Mary Reiner, Stanley Janus, Theresa Janus, Mary McFarland, and Paula Prince.

There were seven victims.

Father Witmer cannot find John Kwiat.

Seven victims.

He cannot find a death notice for a John Kwiat in the state of Illinois in 1982.

Other Google combinations tell him that in 2015, there are more than 3,000 people in the United States who are named John Kwiat or something fairly close or similar. None of a possible right age in Schaumburg, nor in the Northwest Suburbs of Illinois.

Perhaps more dogged and learned researchers could learn more, but Father Witmer decides it is profitless to continue.

Father Witmer sinks to his knees.

Father Witmer prays. He prays late into the night and fears he will find no feeling of relief or validation with the morning.

Father Witmer prays: Lord, I believe; help my unbelief!

THE OLD MAN AND THE DEAD

I

In our time there was a man who wrote as well and truly as anyone ever did. He wrote about courage and endurance and sadness and war and bullfighting and boxing and men in love and men without women. He wrote about scars and wounds that never heal.

Often, he wrote about death. He had seen much death. He had killed. Often, he wrote well and truly about death. Sometimes. Not always.

Sometimes he could not.

II
May 1961
Mayo Clinic
Rochester, Minnesota

"Are you a Stein? Are you a Berg?" he asked.

"Are you an anti-Semite?" the psychiatrist asked.

"No." He thought. "Maybe. I don't know. I used to be, I think. It was in fashion. It was all right until that son of a bitch Hitler."

"Why did you ask that?" the psychiatrist asked.

The old man took off his glasses. He was not really an old man, only sixty-one, but often he thought of himself as an old man and truly, he looked like an old man, although his blood pressure was in control and his diabetes remained borderline. His face had scars. His eyes were sad. He looked like an old man who had been in wars.

He pinched his nose above the bridge. He wondered if he were doing it to look tired and worn. It was hard to know now when he was being himself and when he was being what the world expected him to be. That was how it was when all the world knew you and all the world knows you if you have been in *Life* and *Esquire*.

"It's I don't think a Jew would understand. Maybe a Jew couldn't."

The old man laughed then but it had nothing funny to it. He sounded like he had been socked a good one. "*Nu?* Is that what a Jew would say? *Nu?* No, not a Jew. Not a communist. Nor an empiricist. I'll tell you who else. The existentialists. Those wise guys sons of bitches. Oh, they get ink these days, don't they? Sit in the café's and drink the good wine and the good dark coffee and smoke the bad cigarettes and think they've discovered it all. Nothingness. That is what they think they've discovered. How do you like it now, Gentlemen?

"They are wrong. Yes. They are wrong."

"How so?"

"There is something. It's not pretty. It's not nice. You have to be drunk to talk about it, drunk or shell-shocked, and then you usually can't talk about it. But there is something."

III

The poet Bill Wantling wrote of him: "He explored the *pues y nada* and the *pues y nada.*"

So then so. What do you know of it, Mr. Poet Wantling? What do you know of it?

F___ you all. I obscenity in the face of the collective wisdom. I obscenity in the face of the collective wisdoms. I obscenity in the mother's milk that suckled the collective wisdoms. I obscenity in the too easy mythos of all the collective wisdoms and in the face of my young, ignorant, unknowing self that led me to proclaim my personal mantra of ignorance, the *pues y nada y pues y nada y pues y nada pues y nada* ... In the face of Buddha. In the face of Mohammed. In the face of the God of Abraham, Isaac, and Jacob.

In the face of that poor skinny dreamer who died on

the cross. Really, when it came down to it, he had some good moves in there. He didn't go out bad. He was tough. Give him that. Tough like Stan Ketchel, but he had no counter-moves. Just this sweet, simple, sad-ass faith. Sad-ass because, what little he understood, no, from what I have seen, he had it bass-ackwards.

How do you like it now, Gentlemen? How do you like it now? Is it time for a prayer? Very well then, Gentlemen.

Let us pray.

Baa-baa-baa, listen to the lambs bleat,

Baa-baa-baa, listen to the lambs bleat.

Truly, world without end.

Truly.

Not

Amen.

I can not will not just cannot no cannot bless nor sanctify nor affirm the obscenity the horror.

Can you, Mr. Poet Bill Wantling? Can you, Gentlemen?

How do you like it now?

In Hell and in a time of hell, a man's got no bloody chance, F___ you as we have been f___ed. All of us. All of us.

There is your prayer.

Amen.

IV

"Ern—"

"No. Don't call me that. That's not who I want to be."

"That is your name."

"Goddamn it. F___ you. F___ you twice. I've won the big one. The goddamn Nobel. I'm the one. The heavyweight champ, no middleweight. I *can* be *who* I want to be. I've earned that."

"Who is it you want to be?"

"*Mr. Papa*. I'm damned good for that. Mr. Papa. That is how I call myself. That is how Mary calls me. They call me 'Mr. Papa' in Idaho and Cuba and *Paris Review*. The little girls whose tight dancer bottoms I pinch, the little girls I call 'daughter,' the lovely little girls, and A.E. and Carlos and Coop and Marlene, *Papa* or *Mr. Papa*, that's how they call me.

"Even Fidel. I'm Mr. Papa to Fidel. I call him *Señor Beisbol*. Do you know, he's got a hell of a slider, Fidel? How do you like it now, Mr. Doctor? *Mr.* Papa."

"*Mr. Papa?* No, I don't like it. I don't like the word games you play with me, nor do I think your 'Mr. Papa' role belongs in this office. You're here so we can *help* you."

"Help me? That is nice. That is just so goddamn pretty."

"We need the truth."

"That's all Pilate wanted. Not so much. And wasn't he one swell guy?"

"Who are you?" persisted the psychiatrist.

"Who's on first?"

"What?"

"*What's* on second! Who's on first. I like them, you know. Abbott and Costello. They could teach that sissy Capote a thing or two about word dance. Who's on first? How do you like it now, Gentlemen? Oh, yes, they could teach Mr. James Jones a little. Thinks he's Captain Steel Balls now. Thinks he's ready to go against the champ. Mailer, the loud mouth Hebe. Uris, even *Uris*, for God's sake, the original Hollywood piss-ant. Before they take me on, any of them, let them do a prelim with Abbott and Costello. Who's on first? That is good."

"What's not good is that you're avoiding. Simple question." The psychiatrist was silent, then he said, sternly, "Who are you?"

The old man said nothing. His mouth worked. He looked frail then. Finally he said, "Who am I truly?"

"Truly."

"*Verdad?*"

"*Si. Verdad.*"

"Call me *Adam* ..."

"*Adam?* Oh, *Mr. Papa, Mr. Nobel Prize,* that is just too pretty. How do *you* like it now, thrown right back at you? You see, I can talk your talk. Let us have a pretension contest. Call me 'Ishmael.' Now do we wait for God to call you his beloved son in whom he is well pleased?"

The old man sighed. He looked very sad, as though he wanted to kill himself. He had put himself on his honor to his personal physician and his wife that he would not kill himself, and honor was very important to him, but he looked like he wanted to kill himself.

The old man said, "No. Adam. Adam Nichols. That was the one who was truly me in the stories."

"I thought it was Nick Adams in ..."

"*Those* were the stories I let them publish. There were other stories I wrote about me when I used to be Adam Nichols. Some of those stories no one would have published. Believe me. Maybe *Weird Tales*. Some magazine for boys who don't yet know about f___ing.

"Those stories, they were the real stories."

V
A DANCE WITH A NUN

Adam Nichols had the bed next to his friend Rinelli in the attic of the villa that had been taken over for a hospital and with the war so far off they usually could not even hear it. It was not too bad. It was a small room, the only one for patients all the way up there, and so just the two of them had the room. When you opened the window, there was usually a pleasant breeze that cleared away the smell of dead flesh.

Adam would have been hurting plenty but every time the pain came they gave him morphine and so it wasn't so bad. He had been shot in the calf and the hip and near to the spine and the doctor had to do a lot of cutting. The doctor told him he would be fine. Maybe he wouldn't be able to telemark when he skied, but he would be all right, without even a limp.

The doctor told him about a concert violinist who'd lost his left hand. He told him about a gallery painter who'd been blinded in both eyes. He told him about an ordinary fellow who'd lost both testicles. The doctor said Adam had reason to count his blessings. He was trying to cheer Adam up. Hell, the doctor said, trying to show he was a regular guy who would swear, there were lots had it worse, plenty worse.

Rinelli had it worse. You didn't have to be a doctor to know that. A machine gun got Rinelli in the stomach and in the legs and in between. The machine gun really hem-stitched him. They changed his bandages every hour or so but there was always a thick wetness coming right through the blanket.

Adam Nichols thought Rinelli was going to die because Rinelli said he didn't feel badly at all and they weren't giving him morphine or anything much else really. Another thing was Rinelli laughed and joked a great deal. Frequently, Rinelli said he was feeling "swell"; that was an American word Adam had taught him and Rinelli liked it a lot.

Rinelli joked plenty with Sister Katherine, one of the nurses. He teased hell out of her. She was an American nun and very young and very pretty with sweet blue eyes that made Adam think of the girls with Dutch bobs and round collars who wore silly hats who you saw in the Coca-Cola advertisements. When he first saw her, Rinelli said to Adam Nichols in Italian, "What a waste. What a shame. Isn't she a great girl? Just swell."

There was also a much older nun there called Sister Anne. She was a chief nurse and this was not her first war. Nobody joked with her even if he was going to die. What Rinelli said about her was that when she was a child she decided to be a bitch and because she wasn't British, the only thing left was for her to be a nun. Sister Anne had a profile as flat as the blade of a shovel. Adam told Rinelli he'd put his money on Sister Anne in a twenty-rounder with Jack Johnson. She had to have a harder coconut than any nigger.

Frequently, it was Sister Katherine who gave Adam his morphine shot. With her help, he had to roll onto his side so she could jab the hypodermic into his buttock. That was usually when Rinelli would start teasing.

"Sister Katherine," Rinelli might say, "when you are finished looking at Corporal Nichols's backside, would you be interested in seeing mine?"

"No, no thank you," Sister Katherine would say.

"It needs your attention, Sister. It is broken, I am afraid. It is cracked right down the middle."

"Please, Sergeant Rinelli—"

"Then if you don't want to see my backside, could I perhaps interest you in my front side?"

Sister Katherine would blush very nicely then and do something so young and sweet with her mouth that it was all you could do not to just squeeze her. But then Rinelli would get to laughing and you'd see the bubbles in the puddle on the blanket over his belly, and that wasn't any too nice.

One afternoon, Rinelli casually asked Sister Katherine, "Am I going to live?" Adam Nichols knew Rinelli was not joking then.

Sister Katherine nodded. "Yes," she said. "You are going to get well and then you will go back home."

"No," Rinelli said, still sounding casual, "Pardon me, I really don't want to contradict, but no, I do not think so."

Adam Nichols did not think so, either, and he had been watching Sister Katherine's face so he thought she did not think so as well.

Sister Katherine said rather loudly, "Oh, yes, Sergeant Rinelli. I have talked with the doctors. Yes, I have. Soon you will begin to be better. It will be a gradual thing, you will see. Your strength will come back. Then you can be invalided home."

With his head turned, Adam Nichols saw Rinelli smile.

"Good," Rinelli said. "That is very fine. So, Sister Katherine, as soon as I am better and my strength comes back to me, but before I am sent home, I have a favor to ask of you."

"What is that, Sergeant Rinelli?"

"I want you to dance with me."

Sister Katherine looked youngest when she was trying to be deeply serious. "No, no," she said, emphatically. "No, it is not permitted. Nuns cannot dance."

"It will be a secret dance. I will not tell Sister Anne, have no fear. But I do so want to dance with you."

"Rest now, Sergeant Rinelli. Rest, Corporal Nichols. Soon everything will be fine."

"Oh, yes," Rinelli said, "soon everything will be just swell."

What Adam Nichols liked about morphine was that it was better than getting drunk because you could slip from what was real to what was not real and not know and not care one way or the other. Right now in his mind, he was up in Michigan. He was walking through the woods, following the trail. Ahead, it came into sight, the trout pool, and his eyes took it all in, and he was seeking the words so he could write this moment truly.

Beyond this trail
a stream lies
faintly marked by rising mist.

Twisting and tumbling
around barriers,
it flows
into a shimmering pool,

black with beauty
and
full of fighting trout.

Adam Nichols had not told many people about this writing thing, how he believed he would discover a way to make words present reality so it was not just reality but more real than reality. He wanted writing to jump into what he called the fifth dimension. But until he learned to do it, and for now, writing was a secret for him.

The war was over. Sometimes he tried to write about it but he usually could not. Too often when he would try to write about it, he would find himself writing about what other men had seen and done and not what he himself had seen and done and had to give it up as a bad job.

Adam Nichols put down his tackle and rod and sat down by the pool and lit a cigarette. It tasted good. There is a clean, clear and sharp smell when you light a cigarette outdoors. He was not surprised to find Rinelli sitting alongside him even though Rinelli was dead. Rinelli was smoking, too.

"Isn't this fine? Isn't this everything I said it would be?" Adam Nichols asked.

"It's grand, it sure is. It's just swell," Rinelli answered.

"Tonight, we'll drink some whiskey with really cold water. And we'll have one hell of a meal," Adam Nichols said. "Trout. I've got my old man's recipe." He drew reflectively on his cigarette. "My old man, he was the one who taught me to hunt and fish. He was the one taught me to cook outdoors."

"You haven't introduced me to your father," Rinelli said.

"Well, he's dead, you see. He was a doctor and he killed himself. He put his gun to his head and he killed himself."

"What do you figure, then? Figure he's in hell now?"

"I don't know. Tell you, Rinelli, I don't really think there's anything like that. Hell. Not really."

Rinelli looked sad and that's when Adam Nichols saw how dead Rinelli's eyes were and remembered all over again that Rinelli was dead.

"Well, Adam, you know me, I don't like to argue, but I tell you, there is, too, a hell. And I sure as hell wish I were there right now."

Rinelli snapped the last half inch of his cigarette into the trout pool. A small fish bubbled at it as the trout pool turned into blood.

A few days later Rinelli was pretty bad off. Sometimes he tried to joke with Adam but he didn't make any sense and sometimes he talked in Italian to people who weren't there. He looked gray, like a dirty sheet. When he fell asleep, there was a heavy, wet rattle in his throat and his mouth stayed open.

Adam Nichols wasn't feeling any too swell himself. It was funny, how when you were getting better, you hurt lots worse. Sister Katherine jabbed a lot of morphine into him. It helped, but he still hurt and he knew he wasn't always thinking straight.

There were times he thought he was probably crazy because of the pain and the morphine. That didn't bother him really. It was just that he couldn't trust anything he saw.

At dusk, Adam Nichols opened his eyes. He saw Sister Katherine by Rinelli's bed. She had her crucifix and she was praying hard and quiet with her lips moving prettily and her eyes almost closed.

"That's good," Rinelli said. "Thank you. That is real nice." His voice sounded strong and casual and vaguely bored.

Sister Katherine kept on praying.

"That's just swell," Rinelli said. He coughed and he died.

Sister Katherine pulled the sheets up over Rinelli's face. She went to Adam. "He's gone."

"Well, I guess so."

"We will not be able to move him for a while. We do not have enough people, and there's no room ..." Sister Katherine looked like she had something unpleasant in her mouth. "There is no room in the room we're using for the morgue."

"That's okay," Adam Nichols said. "He can stay here. He's not bothering me."

"All right then," Sister Katherine said. "All right. Do you need another shot of morphine?"

"Yes," Adam said, "I think so. I think I do."

Sister Katherine gave him the injection, and later there was another, and then, he thought, perhaps another one or even two. He knew he had had a lot of morphine because what he saw later was really crazy and couldn't have actually happened.

It was dark and Sister Katherine came in with her little light. Rinelli sat up in bed then. That had to be the morphine, Adam Nichols told himself. Rinelli was dead as a post. But there he was, sitting up in bed, with dead eyes, and he was stretching out his arms and then it all happened quick just like in a dream but Rinelli was out of bed and he was hugging Sister Katherine like he was drunk and silly.

He's dancing with her, that's what he's doing, Adam Nichols thought, and he figured he was thinking that because of all the morphine. Sure, he said he was going to dance with Sister Katherine before he went home. "Hey, Rinelli," Adam Nichols said. "Quit fooling around, why don't you?"

Sister Katherine was yelling pretty loud and then she wasn't yelling all that loud because it looked like Rinelli was kissing her, but then you saw that wasn't it. Rinelli was biting her nose real hard, not like kidding around, and she was bleeding pretty much and she twisted and pushed real hard on Rinelli.

Rinelli staggered back. With blood on his dead lips. With something white and red and pulpy getting chewed by his white teeth. With a thin bit of pink gristle by the corner of his mouth.

Sister Katherine was up against the wall. The middle of her face was a black and red gushing hole. Her eyes were real big and popping. She was yelling without making a sound. She kind of looked like a comic strip.

It was a bad dream and the morphine, Adam Nichols thought, a real bad dream, and he wished he'd wake up.

Then Sister Anne came running in. Then she ran out. Then she ran back in. Now she had a Colt .45. She knocked back the slide like she really meant business. Rinelli went for her. She held her arm straight out. The gun was just a few inches from Rinelli's forehead when Sister Anne let him have it. Rinelli's head blew up wetly in a lot of noise. A lot of the noise was shattering bone. It went all over the place.

That was all Adam Nichols could remember the next morning. It wasn't like something real you remember. It was a lot more like a dream. He told himself it had to be the morphine. He told himself that a number of times. The windows were open and the breeze was nice but the small room smelled of strong disinfectant. There was no one in the other bed.

When Sister Anne came in to bring his breakfast and give him morphine, Adam Nichols asked about Rinelli.

"Well, he's dead," Sister Anne said. "I thought you knew."

Adam Nichols asked about Sister Katherine.

"She's no longer here," the old nun said, tersely.

"I thought something happened last night. I thought I saw something awful."

"It's better you don't think about it," Sister Anne said. "It's war and everybody sees a lot of awful things. Just don't think about it."

"Let's talk about your suicidal feelings."

"There are times I want to kill myself. How's that?"

"You know what I mean."

"Who's on first?"

"You pride yourself on being a brave man."

"I am. Buck Lanham called me the bravest man he's ever known."

"Hooray. I'll see you get a medal."

"Maybe I deserve a medal. I've pissed in the face of death." The old man winked then. That and what he had just said made him look ridiculous. It made him look ancient and crazy. "I have killed, after all."

"I know. You are a very famous killer. You have antlers and tusks and rhino horns. You've shot cape buffalo and geese and bears and wild goats. That makes you extremely brave. You deserve medals."

"Who are you to deride me?" The old man was furious. He

looked threatening and silly. "Who are you to hold me in contempt? I have killed men!"

VII

The time is a drunken blur in his memory. It is the "rat race" summer and fall of 1944, and he is intensely alive. A "war correspondent," that is what he is supposed to be, but that is not all he can allow himself to be.

He has to go up against Death every time. With what he knows, oh, yes, he has to meet the flat gaze of Mr. Death, has to breathe Mr. Death's hyena breath, he has to.

That is part of it.

He calls himself a soldier. He wouldn't have it any other way. This is a war. He appoints himself an intelligence officer. He carries a weapon, a .32 caliber Colt revolver.

And don't the kids love him, though? God, he sure loves them. They are just so goddamned beautiful, the doomed ones and the fortunate, the reluctant warriors and those who've come to know they love it. They are beautiful men as only men can be beautiful.

You see, women, well, women are women, and it is the biological thing, the trap by which we are snared, the old peg and awl, the old belly-rub and sigh and there you have it, and so a real man does need a woman, must have a woman so he does not do heinous things, but it is in the company of men that men find themselves and each other.

These kid warriors, these glorious snot-noses like he used to be, they know he is tough. He is the legit goods. He can outshoot them, rifle or pistol, even the Two Gun Pecos Pete from Arizona. Want to play cards, he'll stay up the night, drinking and joking. He puts on the gloves and boxes with them. He'll take one to give one and he always gives as good as he gets.

He has a wind-up phonograph and good records: Harry James and the Boswells and Hot Lips Paige. He has Fletcher Henderson and Basie and Ellington. The Andrews Sisters, they can swing it, and Russ Colombo, Sinatra, he'll be fine once they let him stop doing the sappy stuff. There are nights of music and drinking and in the following days there are the moments burned into his mind, the moments that become the stories. Old man?

Well, he can drink the kids blind-eyed and to hell and gone. He stays with them, drink for drink. The hell with most of the kiss-ass officers. They don't know how foolish they are. They don't know they are clichés. The enlisted men, John Q. Public, Mr. O.K. Joe American, Johnny Gone for a Soldier, it's the enlisted man who's going to save the world from that Nazi bastard. It's the enlisted men he honest to God loves.

The enlisted men call him "Papa."

How do you like it now, Gentlemen?

The kraut prisoner was no enlisted man. He was an officer. Stiff-necked son of a bitch. *Deutschland über alles.* Arrogant pup. *Übermensch.*

No, the German will not reveal anything. He will answer none of their questions. They can all go to hell. That's what the German officer says. They can all get f_____.

Papa shakes a fist in the kraut's face. Papa says, "You're going to talk and tell us every damned thing we want to know or I'll kill you, you Nazi son of a bitch."

The German officer does not change expression. He looks bored. What he says is: "You are not going to kill me, old man. You do not have the courage. You are hindered by a decadent morality and ethical code. You come from a race of mongrelized degenerates and cowards. You abide by the foolishness of the Geneva Convention. I am an unarmed prisoner of war. You will do nothing to me."

Later, he would boastfully write about this incident to the soft-spoken, courtly gentlemen who published his books. He said to the German officer, "What a mistake you made, brother."

> *And then I shot that smug prick. I just shot him before anyone could tell me I shouldn't. I let him have three in the belly, just like that, real quick, from maybe a foot away.*
>
> *Say what you want, maybe they were no supermen, but they weren't any pantywaists. Three in the belly, Pow-Pow-Pow, and he's still standing there, and damned if he isn't dead but doesn't know it, but he is pretty surprised and serves him right, too.*
>
> *Then everyone else, all the Americans and a Brit or two are yelling and pissing around like they don't know whether to shit, go blind, or order breakfast, and here's this dead kraut swaying on his feet, and*

*maybe I'm even thinking I'm in a kettle of bad soup,
but the hell with it.*

*But have to do it right, you know, arrogant
krautkopf or not. So I put the gun to his head and I
let him have it, bang! and his brains come squirting
right out his nose, gray and pink, and, you know, it
looks pretty funny, so someone yells "Gesundheit!"
and that's it, brother. That's all she wrote and we've
got us one guaranteed dead Nazi.*

VIII

A rose is a rose is a rose
The dead are the dead are the dead except when they aren't
and how do you like it
let's talk and
Who is on first
I know what I know and I am afraid and I am afraid

IX
HOMAGE TO SPAIN
1. An Old Man's Luck

The dusty old man sat on the river bank. He wore steel-
rimmed spectacles. He had already traveled twelve kilometers
and he was very tired. He thought it would be a while before he
could go on.

That is what he told Adam Nichols.

Adam Nichols told him he had to cross the pontoon bridge. He
really must and soon. When the shelling came, this would not be
a good place to stay. The old man in the steel-rimmed spectacles
thanked Adam Nichols for his concern. He was a very polite old
man. The reason he had stayed behind was to take care of the
animals in his village. He smiled because saying "his village" made
him feel good. There were three goats, two cats, and six doves.
When he had no other choice and really had to leave, he opened
the door to the doves' cage and let them fly. He was not too
worried about the cats, really, the old man told Adam Nichols;
cats are always all right. Cats had luck. Goats were another thing.
Goats were a little stupid and sweet and so they had not much

luck.

It was just too bad about the goats, the old man said. It was a sad thing.

Adam agreed. But the old man had to move along. He really should.

The old man said thank you. He was grateful for the concern. But he did not think he could go on just yet. He was very tired and he was seventy-six years old.

He asked a question. Did Adam truly think the cats would be all right?

Yes, Adam said, we both know cats have luck.

Adam thought they had a lot more luck than sweet and stupid goats and seventy-six-year-old men who can go no farther than twelve kilometers when there is going to be shelling.

2. Hunters in the Morning Fog

Miguel woke him. They used to call him Miguelito but the older Miguel had been shot right through the heart, a very clean shot, and so now this one was Miguel. The sun had just come up and there was fog with cold puff-like clouds near to the ground. "Your rifle," Miguel said. "We are going hunting."

"Hey," Adam Nichols said, "what the hell?" He wanted coffee or to go back to sleep.

"Just come," Miguel said.

There were five of them, Pilar, who was as tough as any man, and Antonio, and Jordan, the American college professor, and Miguel, who used to be Miguelito, and Adam Nichols. They went out to the field. Yesterday it was a battlefield. The day before that it had just been a green, flat field. Some of the dead lay here and there. Not all of the dead were still. Some were already up and some were now rising, though most lay properly still and dead. Those who were up mostly staggered about like drunks. Some had their arms out in front of them like Boris Karloff in the *Frankenstein* movie. They did not look frightening. They looked stupid. But they were frightening even if they did not look frightening because they were supposed to be dead.

"Say, what the hell?" Adam Nichols asked. His mouth was dry.

"It happens sometimes," Pilar said. "That is what I have heard. It appears to be so, though this is the first time I personally have seen it."

Pilar shrugged. "The dead do not always stay dead. They come back sometimes. What they do then is quite sickening. It is revolting and disgusting. When they come back, they are cannibals. They wish to eat living people. And if they bite you, they cause a sickness, and then you die, and then after that, you become like them and you wish to eat living people. We have to shoot them. A bullet in the head; that is what stops them. It's not so bad, you know. It's not like they are really alive."

"I don't go for this," Adam said.

"Don't talk so much," Pilar said. "I like you very much, *Americano*, but don't talk so much."

She put her rifle to her shoulder. It was an old '03 Springfield. It had plenty of stopping power. Pilar was a good shot. She fired and one of the living dead went down with the middle of his face punched in.

"Come on," Pilar said, commanding. "We stay together. We don't let any of these things get too close. That is what they are. Things. They aren't strong, but if there are too many, then it can be trouble."

"I don't think I like this," Adam Nichols said. "I don't think I like it at all."

"I am sorry, but what you like and what you dislike is not all that important, if you will forgive my saying so," Miguel said. "What does matter is that you are a good shot. You are one of our best shots. So, if you please, shoot some of these unfortunate dead people."

Antonio and Pilar and Jordan and Miguel and Adam Nichols shot the living dead as the hunting party walked through the puffy clouds of fog that lay on the field. Adam felt like his brain was the flywheel in a clock about to go out of control. He remembered shooting black squirrels when he was a boy. Sometimes you shot a black squirrel and it fell down and then when you went to pick it up it tried to bite you and you had to shoot it again or smash its head with a rock or the stock of your rifle. He tried to make himself think this was just like shooting black squirrels. He tried to make himself think it was even easier, really, because dead people moved a lot slower than black squirrels. It was hard to shoot a squirrel skittering up a tree. It was not so hard to shoot a dead man walking like a tired drunk toward you.

Then Adam saw the old man who had sat by the pontoon bridge the other day. The old man's steel-rimmed spectacles hung from one ear. They were unshattered. He looked quite silly, like something in a Chaplin film. Much of his chest had been torn open and bones stuck out at crazy angles. There were wettish tubular like things wrapped about the protruding bones of his chest.

He was coming at Adam Nichols like a trusting drunk who finds a friend and knows the friend will see him home.

"Get that one," said Jordan, the American college professor. "That one is yours."

Yes, Adam Nichols thought, *the old man is mine. We have talked about goats and cats and doves.*

Adam Nichols sighted. He took in a breath and held it. He waited.

The old man stumbled toward him.

Come, old man, Adam Nichols thought. *Come with your chest burst apart and your terrible appetite. Come with the mindless brute insistence that makes you continue. Come to the bullet that will give you at least the lie of a dignified ending. Come unto me, old man. Come unto me.*

"You let him draw too close," Miguel said. "Shoot him now."

Come, old man, Adam Nichols thought. *Come, because I am your luck. Come because I am all the luck you are ever going to have.*

Adam pulled the trigger. It was a fine shot. It took off the top of the old man's head. His glasses flew up and he flew back and lay on the fog-heavy ground.

"Good shot," Jordan said.

"No," Adam said, "just good luck."

3. In A Hole in the Mountain

It is not true that every man in Spain is named Paco, but it is true that if you call "Paco!" on the street of any city in Spain, you will have many more than one "*Qué*" in response.

It was with a Paco whom Adam Nichols found himself hiding from the fascist patrols. Paco's advanced age and formidable mustache made him look *Gitano*. Paco was a good fighter, and a good Spaniard, but not such a good communist. He said he was too old to have politics, but not too old to kill fascists.

Adam Nichols was now a communist because of some papers he had signed. Now he blew up things. For three months, he had been to a special school in Russia to learn demolitions. Adam Nichols was old enough now to know his talents. He was good at teaching young people to speak Spanish, and so for a while he had been a bored and boring high school teacher of Spanish in Oak Park, Illinois. Blowing up things and killing fascists was much more interesting, so he had gone to Spain.

There were other reasons, too. He seldom let himself ponder these.

The previous day, Adam Nichols had blown up a railroad trestle that certain military leaders had agreed was important, and, except for old Paco, the comrades who had made possible this act of demolition were all dead. The fascists were seeking the man who had destroyed the trestle. But Paco knew how to hide.

Where Paco and Adam were hiding was too small to be a cave. It was just a hole in a mountainside. It was hard to spot unless you knew just what you were looking for.

It was dark in the hole. Paco and Adam could not build a fire. But it was safe to talk if you talked in the same low embarrassed way you did in the confessional. Because they were so close, there were times when Adam could almost feel that Paco was breathing for him and that he was breathing for Paco. A moment came to Adam Nichols that made him think, *This is very much like being lovers,* but then he decided it was not so. He would never be as close with a lover as he was now with Paco.

After many hours of being with Paco in the close dark, Adam said, "Paco, there is something I wish to ask thee." Adam Nichols spoke in the most formal Spanish. It was what was needed.

Gravely, though he was not a serious man, Paco said, "Then ask, but remember, Comrade, I am an aged man, and do not mistake age for wisdom." Paco chuckled. He was pleased he had remembered to say "comrade." Sometimes he forgot. It was hard to be a good communist.

"I need to speak of what I have seen. Of abomination. Of horror. Of impossibility."

"Art thou speaking of war?"

"Sí"

"Then dost thou speak of courage, too?" Paco asked. "Of decency? Or self-sacrifice?"

"No, *Viejo,*" Adam Nichols said. "Of these things, much has been said and much written. Courage, decency, self-sacrifice are to be found in peace or war. Stupidity, greed, arrogance are to be found in peace or war. But I wish to speak with thee of that which I have seen only during time of war. It is madness. It is what cannot be."

Paco said, "What wouldst thou ask of me?"

"Paco," Adam Nichols said, "do the dead walk?"

"Hast thou seen this?"

"*Verdad.* I have seen this. No. I think I have seen this. Years ago, a long time back, in that which was my first war, I thought I saw it. It was in that war, Paco *Viejo,* that I think I became a little crazy. And now I think I have seen in it in this war. There were others with me when we went to kill the dead. They would not talk of it, after. After, we all got drunk and made loud toasts which were vows of silence." Adam Nichols was silent for a time. Then he said again, "Do the dead walk?"

"Thou hast good eyes, Comrade Adam. Thou shootest well. Together we have been in battle. Thou dost not become crazy. What thou hast seen, thou hast seen truly."

Adam Nichols was quiet. He remembered when he was a young man and his heart was broken by a love gone wrong and the loss of well-holding arms and a smile that was for no one else but him. He felt worse now, filled with sorrow and fear both, and with his realizing the world was such a serious place. He said, "It is a horrible thing when the dead walk."

"*Verdad.*"

"Dost thou understand what happens?"

"Perhaps."

"Then perhaps you can tell me."

"Perhaps." Paco sighed. His sigh seemed to move the darkness in waves. "Years ago, I knew a priest. He was not a fascist priest. He was a nice man. The money in his plate did not go to buy candlesticks. He built a motion picture theater for his village. He knew that you need to laugh on Saturdays more than you need stained glass windows. The movies he showed were very good movies. Buster Keaton. Harold Lloyd. Joe Bonomo. John Gilbert.

KoKo the Klown and Betty Boop cartoons. This priest did not give a damn for politics, he told me. He gave a damn about people. And that is the reason, I believe, that he stopped being a priest. He had some money. He had three women who loved him and were content to share him. I think he was all right, this priest.

"It was he who told me of the living dead."

"And canst thou tell me?"

"Well, yes, I believe I can. There is no reason not to. I have sworn no oaths."

"What is it, then? Why do the dead rise? Why do they seek the flesh of the living?"

"This man who had been a priest was not certain about Heaven, but he was most definite about Hell. Yes, Hell was the Truth. Hell was for the dead.

"But when we turn this Earth of ours into Hell, there is no need for the dead to go below.

"Why should they bother?

"And canst thou doubt that much of this ball of mud upon which we dwell is today hell, Comrade? With each new war and each new and better way of making war, there is more and more hell and so we have more and more inhabitants of hell with us.

"And of course, no surprise, they have their hungers. They are demons. At least that is what some might call them, though I myself seldom think to call them anything. And the food of demons is human flesh. It is a simple thing, really."

"Paco—"

"*Sí?*"

"This is not rational."

"And art thou a rational man?"

"Yes. No."

"So?"

"'The Living Dead,' maybe that's what somebody would call them. Well, hell, don't you think that would make some newspaperman just ecstatic? It would be bigger than 'Lindy in Paris!' Bigger than—"

"And thou dost believe such a newspaper story could be printed? And perhaps the *Book of the Living Dead* could be written? And perhaps a motion picture of the Living Dead as well, with Buster Keaton, perhaps? Comrade Adam, such revelation would topple the world order.

"Perhaps someday the world will be ready for such awful knowledge, Comrade Adam.

"For now, it is more than enough that those of us who know of it must know of it, thank you very kindly.

"And with drink and with women and with war and with whatever gives us comfort, we must try not to think over much about what it is we know."

"Paco," Adam Nichols said in the dark, "I think I want to scream. I think I want to scream now."

"No, Comrade. Be quiet now. Breathe deep. Breathe with me and deep. Let me breathe for you. Be quiet."

"All right," Adam said after a time. "It is all right now."

A day later, Paco thought it would be safe to leave the hole in the side of the mountain. They were spotted by an armored car full of fascists. A bullet passed through Paco's lung. It was a mortal shot.

"Bad luck, Paco," Adam Nichols said. He put a bullet into the old man's brain and went on alone.

X

"You're really not helping me. You know that."

"Bad on me. I thought I was here for you to help me. My foolishness. Damn the luck."

"I've decided, then, we'll go the way we did before, with electro-convulsive therapy. We'll …

I am for god's sake sixty-one years old and I am going to die because of occluded arteries or because of a cirrhotic liver or because of an aneurysm in brain or belly waiting to go pop, or because of some damn thing—and when I die I wish to be dead to be dead and that is all.

"—a series of twelve. We've often had good results—"

and, believe me, I am not asking for Jesus to make me a sunbeam, I am not asking for heaven in any way, shape, or form. Gentlemen, when I die I wish to be dead.

"—particularly with depression. There are several factors, of course—"

I'm looking for dead, that's D-E-A-D, and I don't want to be a goddamn carnival freak show act and man is just a little lower than the angels and pues y nada *and you get older and you get confused and you become afraid.*

"We'll begin tomorrow—"

no bloody chance because now the world is hell and if you doubt it, then you don't know the facts, Gentlemen. No bloody chance. We ended the war by dropping hell on Nagasaki and on Hiroshima, and we opened up Germany and discovered all those hells, and during the siege of Stalingrad, the living ate the dead, and ta-ta, Gentlemen, turnabout is fair play, and we're just starting to know the hells that good old Papa Joe put together no bloody chance and we're not blameless, oh, no, ask that poor nigger hanging burning from the tree, ask the Rosenbergs who got cooked up nice and brown, ask—Welcome to hell, and how do you like it now, Gentlemen?

When the world is hell, the dead walk.

XI

When they returned to Ketchum, Idaho on June 30, the old man was happy. Anyone who saw him will tell you. He was not supposed to drink because of his anti-depressant medication, but he did drink. It did not affect him badly. He sang several songs. One was "*La Quince Brigada*," from the Spanish Civil War. He sang loudly and off-key; he made a joyful racket. He said one of the great regrets of his life was that he had never learned to play the banjo.

Later, he had his wife, Mary, put on a Burl Ives record on the Webcor phonograph. It was a seventy-eight: "The Riddle Song." He listened to it several times.

> *How can there be a cherry*
> *that has no stone?*
> *How can there be a chicken*
> *that has no bone?*
> *How can there be a baby*
> *with no crying?*

Mary asked if the record made him sad.

No, he said, he was not sad at all. The record was beautiful. If there are riddles, there are also answers to riddles.

So, so then, I have not done badly. Some good stories, some good books. I have written well and truly. I have sometimes failed, but I have tried. I have sometimes been a foolish man, and even a small-minded or mean-spirited one, but I have always been a man, and I will end as a man.

It was early and he was the only one up. The morning of Sunday, July 2, was beautiful. There were no clouds. There was sunshine.

He went to the front foyer. He liked the way the light struck the oak-paneled walls and the floor. It was like being in a museum or in a church. It was a well-lighted place and it felt clean and airy.

Carefully, he lowered the butt of the Boss shotgun to the floor. He leaned forward. The twin barrels were cold circles in the scarred tissue just above his eyebrows.

He tripped both triggers.

LIGHT

Because you know the story, you might see in the photograph an element of drama, perhaps even pathos.
That is only your thought, your projection onto this banal image.
A washed-out snapshot.
Hard to judge the light. You cannot tell if it is a sunny day.
She seems a sunny child.
She is three years old.
She wears a striped bathing suit.
Her eyes do not squint.
It is you she sees.
Her mouth is as wide as the blade of a toy shovel.
Unattractive, really.
She holds out her arms.
Does she want you to pick her up, embrace her, take her away?
Is she asking, —Will you love me?
—Will you love me?
—Will you love me?
Because you know the story ...

"Ever since I can remember, I've wanted to be a movie star. I love the movies. When I was a little girl, it seemed the only time I was alive was when I was at the movies. The movies were much more real to me than life."
– Marilyn Monroe

August 4, 1962
Marilyn Monroe's bedroom
Los Angeles

Marilyn Monroe lies naked and dying.

Respiration: Shallow and irregular.

Blue-fade-to-black above the half-moons of her fingernails.

Eyelids seem to thicken as you watch.

Pasty white drool at the left corner of her mouth.

But if you look very hard, there is an almost imperceptible shimmering. Faint, like a trick of weary eyes.

Not rising from her but settling about her.

Light.

June 6, 1930
Los Angeles

Norma Jeane walks into the theater.

Gladys is taking her to the movies.

Gladys is crazy.

But there are times when the mouse-hole voices whisper softly, softly without threat, almost lulling.

Times when staircase men (they can appear *just like that!*) do not seek to punish her for bad thinkings.

Times like now. Hey, Sport, maybe Gladys seems a bit dingy but in a cute kind of way.

No danger to herself or others:

Gracie Allen, not Lizzie Borden.

Today, Gladys and Norma Jeane go to The New Electric Theater. One o'clock show. The New Electric was new back when Tillie's Romance got punctured. It's a ten-cent, third-run, stale-popcorn movie house.

Fair number of people at the show.

No late checks here. A dime can buy shelter for a good part of the day. Gladys and Norma Jeane sit as far as possible from everyone else.

You have to be careful. Not just careful, but *extra* careful when you are crazy.

Gladys offers popcorn to Norma Jeane.

No butter. Too easy for them to put secret chemicals in melted butter.

Norma Jeane does not want popcorn.

Gladys leans toward her. Her eyes glitter. —You should take the popcorn. I want you to be happy.

Norma Jeane smells the lie and craziness on her mother's breath. She takes popcorn. She wishes she were away from here. Wishes she were safe.

She will wish this many more times in her life.

On the screen ... Cartoon. Dancing hippos, elephants, bears. Dots inside circles for bellybuttons. Screechy chorus and xylophone.

Norma Jeane cranes neck way back. Presses the crown of her head into the seat.

Above, projector beams. Columns and cones and fingers of light, yellow-white-clear, criss-crossing, splitting and uniting.

Pathways in the darkness.

Light.

It is beautiful.

On screen: Man with stiff arm out. Looks silly. Silly name: *Doo-chee. DOO-Chee.*

Makes Norma Jeane think of poop.

Norma Jeane laughs.

Gladys sinks fingernails into Norma Jeane's neck. —You must not laugh so loud. They will hear you. Learn to laugh a secret laugh. Inside.

On the screen: A beautiful woman. She is a radiance. She is a luminosity.

Oh! Norma Jeane can hardly breathe, she is so beautiful.

The radiance of the beautiful woman fills her eyes.

She wants to laugh and to cry.

—Laugh on the inside. Cry on the inside.

Gladys tells her: —That is Jean Harlow.

Gladys tells her: —She is the most beautiful woman in the world.

Norma Jeane thinks: *Beautiful, beautiful, beautiful ...*

Gladys whispers: —*Her* name is *Jean* Harlow. *Your* name is Norma *Jeane.*

Gladys whispers: —Jean Harlow, Norma Jeane. Your momma knows what she's doing. Your momma has a *plan.*

Norma Jeane hears crazy. Looks at Jean Harlow, the most beautiful woman in the world. Looks only at Jean Harlow.

—Look at her.

Gladys says it crazy.

Gladys takes her ear and twists it.

Norma Jeane says a secret *Ow!* inside herself.

—Look at her! A command and threat.

Norma Jeane cranks back her neck.

—You can be her. You will be her.

Pain.

Stares upward.

Above, edge-melding beams of light. Of light.

The light goes to the screen.

The light becomes Jean Harlow.

Norma Jeane did not know her father. Gladys did not know him, either. Not for certain. Growing up, Norma Jeane fantasized: Clark Gable was her father. Later, Howard Hughes. Later, Ernest Hemingway. *Papa.*

(When she became Marilyn Monroe, a world renowned psychiatrist told her many of her problems stemmed from a lifelong search for a father.

(—Well, she said, I was wondering. Guess that takes care of that.)

Norma Jeane had a dog. Tippy. Tippy barked. A neighbor did not like the noise. He was a round-faced man with a tattoo. He chopped Tippy in half with a hoe.

Norma Jeane is staying with Aunt Grace. (Gladys is ... *sick*. Your mother is in the hospital because she is sick ... Cuu-koo! Cuu-koo!)

Aunt Grace has a boarder. A man.

He gives Norma Jeane a Sen-Sen. She does not like Sen-Sen but she takes it.

The man says he likes her.

She likes it when people like her. She wants everyone to like her.

—Come here. You are beautiful.

She likes being called beautiful.
The man touches her.
—Beautiful little girl.
Norma Jeane does not like his touching.
The man frightens her.
—Beautiful, the man tells her.
—I will tell, Norma Jeane says.
—Who will you tell? the man says.
—A policeman.
—Aunt Grace.
—Jesus in the sky.
The man laughs.
—Then give me some more Sen-Sen, she says.
—And a nickel.

Norma Jeane Baker Mortenson: To the Los Angeles Orphan Home Society she was Orphan 3463.
—Be good, Aunt Grace told her and abandoned her.
Norma Jeane could not stop crying. Not inside crying. She told them and she told them ... *She was* not *an orphan.* She had a mother!
(Her mother was in the crazy house. Her mother was smelling bad smells and listening to the radio without a radio and making plans. And if *she* did not stop crying, they would think she was crazy like her mother and guess what happens then ...)
—Stop crying.
—Now!
She began to change.
She smiled.
She became a good girl.
They would like that. They would like her.
She was acting.
Years later, when she was Marilyn Monroe, she would meet Katharine Hepburn. It was a brief, public meeting. The press was there. She was a starlet becoming a star. She was expected to say something sexy.
She said, —Sex is part of nature. I go along with nature.
Katharine Hepburn said, —Acting is a nice childish profession-

pretending you're someone else and, at the same time, selling yourself.

She decided she did not like Katharine Hepburn.

Katharine Hepburn understood her.

———

"Looking back, I guess I used to play-act all the time. For one thing, it meant I could live in a more interesting world than the one around me."
– Marilyn Monroe

Norma Jeane hated Vine Elementary School. Had to march there with all the children from the Home on El Centro. It was Orphans on Parade. Everyone looked at you.

Reading was hard then. She mixed up words. She stuttered.

(Muh-muh my *nn*-name is Nuh-*nn*-NormaJean!)

Norma Jeane was in the low reading group: Bluebirds were best. Yellowbirds were next. Then you had Blackbirds. Blackbirds were stupid. Norma Jeane was the only girl Blackbird. The rest were boys. Boys did not mind being Blackbirds. They would not have minded being Buzzards or Turkeys.

(Later, Marilyn Monroe would love reading. She would read Sartre and Joyce and Shaw and Fitzgerald. She would read Hemingway and want very much to meet him. She would read American poets. Carl Sandburg—she did meet him—and Edgar Lee Masters were her favorites.)

Norma Jeane skipped school one day. She went to the movies. She went even though she knew she would get in trouble.

She saw a Bosko cartoon and a Fox Movietone newsreel and a movie called *Sea of Dreams* and a Laurel and Hardy movie. Laurel was the skinny one. Hardy was the fat one. They had a piano to push up a long flight of stairs. The heavy piano made a painful noise on each step. Then the piano fell down all the stairs. They had to shove it all the way back up. Then they learned there was a road they could have used so ... They carried it back down the stairs!

Laurel and Hardy were funny and sad. They reminded you of everybody.

Then the movies were finished.

161

Norma Jeane did not want to leave.

She knew she was in serious trouble.

So she stayed.

The movies started again.

That was how it worked.

She got tired.

She leaned way back in her seat and looked up.

Pathways of light.

Then Stan Laurel is in the seat alongside her. He takes off his derby and balances it on his knee.

She is not surprised. She is glad.

—I had a dream that I was awake and I woke up to find myself asleep, Stan Laurel says.

She knows what he means.

—I'm in trouble, Norma Jeane tells him.

—Neither do I, too, Stan Laurel says.

—That's silly, Norma Jeane says. —That's funny.

—Why yes, Stan Laurel says. —You can lead a horse to water, but a pencil must be led.

He smiles and slowly fades away, becoming glimmering dust motes that rise and swirl into the light streams above.

It is almost sunset when Norma Jeane returns to the Los Angeles Orphan Home.

—We were all quite concerned, Miss Daltrey, the assistant director said, recalling the incident some years later.

—Once we knew she was all right, I was going to punish her ...

—Then she started, well, whimpering, whimpering in a high-pitched voice. She scrunched up her little face and her mouth stretched and turned down—really, it was like the mask of tragedy, a crescent, and she was scratching the top of her head and blinking both eyes in slow motion ....

—This is another fine *mm*-meh-mess I've gotten myself into, is what she said.

—She was *just* like him, you know, the skinny one, and Norma Jeane stuttered, and you certainly did not *want* to laugh at that, but it was just so funny. I let her off with two extra days drying dishes. There was a shine to our Norma Jeane. I remember thinking she was a natural talent and that she would become a *comédienne* like Carole Lombard or Jean Harlow.

Funds were a problem. No Christmas tree in the Orphan Home. Norma Jeane decided a tree would be delivered by Santa Claus. She made up a song and sang it. (She did not stammer when she sang.)

> *Santa will bring me a Christmas Tree*
> *A long red scarf,*
> *and an apple pie ...*
> *Santa will bring me a Christmas Tree—*
> *and oh, how happy I will be!*

The other children made fun of Norma Jeane. Even the real little kids knew Santa Claus was not real. It was the Depression.

Norma Jeane made up a new song.

> *Jesus will bring me a Christmas Tree*
> *A long red scarf,*
> *and an apple pie ...*
> *Jesus will bring me a Christmas Tree*
> *and take me to heaven when I die!*

August 4, 1962
Marilyn Monroe's bedroom

Marilyn Monroe is dying.

Her diaphragm has quit working and her breathing is now all from the stomach. Her skin has a bluish cast and if you were to take her wrist, you might find her pulse only with difficulty.

In this dark room, with no one to see, points of light, little stars, are gathering.

A glowing dome of light covers her.

"We are all of us stars, and we deserve to twinkle."
– Marilyn Monroe

June 7, 1937

Jean Harlow died. Age: twenty-six.
June 26, 1937

Norma Jeane left the orphanage. Now Aunt Grace *would* take
her in.

Norma Jeane stood in front of the Los Angeles Orphans Home
Society. She wished she had a derby to tip in farewell.

A thought came to her and she remembered it—exactly—
years later.

—I had the strange feeling I was being set free into a world in
which Jean Harlow no longer lived.

Then she got in Aunt Grace's Buick and went home.

———

> "Jean Harlow ... I kept thinking of her, rolling over
> the facts of her life in my mind. It was kind of
> spooky, and sometimes I thought, am I making this
> happen? But I don't think so. We just seemed to
> have the same spirit or something, I don't know. I
> kept wondering if I would die young like her, too."
> – Marilyn Monroe

Saturday, July 24, 1937

Norma Jeane waited in the long line at Grauman's Chinese.
The film, *Saratoga*, had been released the previous day.

It starred Clark Gable and Jean Harlow.

It was Jean Harlow's final film.

Norma Jeane watched the movie.

And without watching—not exactly—she seemed constantly
aware of shifting waves of light above.

June 19, 1942

Norma Jeane married the boy next door. Nice guy: Jim
Dougherty. She was sixteen. He was twenty-three. She married
him to stay out of the orphanage. (Aunt Grace could not keep her

any longer.) Jim married Norma Jeane because he was a nice guy.

That's part of it: there were other reasons.

Jim was away for a long time with the Merchant Marine.

Norma Jeane had a factory job but she was pretty and had a va-va-voom figure. She soon got other jobs: modeling in shorts and skimpy tops and bathing suits. She did one picture looking back over her shoulder like Betty Grable. Her smile was not as perfect as Betty Grable's but her *tush* was better than Betty Grable's.

Lots of guys saw pictures like that of Norma Jeane in *Wink* and *Laff* and *Picture Parade* and *Caper* and *Gala*.

Nice guy Jim did not like all the guys looking at photographs of Norma Jeane's *tush*.

So they got divorced.

"I used to think as I looked out on the Hollywood night there must be thousands of girls sitting alone like me, dreaming of becoming a movie star. But I'm not going to worry about them. I'm dreaming the hardest."
– Marilyn Monroe

Norma Jeane posed nude.
Calendar Girl.
Marilyn in the flesh on swirls of red velvet.
Photographer Tom Kelley had no problem with lighting.
She glowed.
Tom Kelley called the picture *Golden Dreams.*
He understood.

"I'm going to be a great movie star some day."
– Marilyn Monroe

And so:
Got a nose job.

Gave some blow jobs.
Changed her name.
Marilyn Monroe.
Muh-Muh-Marilyn Monroe.
—No, goddamnit! Marilyn goddamnit Monroe goddamnit.
Unbilled extra.
—How about a tumble?
Extra. Two days.
Took voice lessons.
Took acting lessons.
Marilyn Monroe.
Walk-on.
Chorus girl in *Love Happy* with Harpo and Groucho Marx.
Banged Groucho.
Banged Harpo.
John Carroll (B movie star) and his wife Lucille (Director, Talent Department, MGM). Three way.
Banged Joe Schenck. (Chairman, 20th Century Fox.)
Banged Harry Cohn (President, Columbia Pictures.)
Banged Johnny Hyde. She called him "the kindest man in the world."
Johnny Hyde said —Marry me. I've got a bad heart. I'll croak soon, leave you fixed like the Queen of the Nile and not a *nafke*.
She said —No.
He died.
Second billing in *Ladies of the Chorus.*
Tah-dah!
She got to act. She got to sing.
She sang "Every Baby Needs a Daddy."
You know, all in all, it did not take that long.
Not really.
Marilyn Monroe was becoming a star.

"Success came to me in a rush ... all the movie magazines and newspapers started printing my picture and giving me write-ups."
– Marilyn Monroe

1952

Monkey Business.
20th Century Fox.
Cary Grant. Ginger Rogers. A chimpanzee named Esther.
Second billing: Marilyn Monroe.
Cast as a secretary named Lois LaVerne.
—You'll have to be funny.
—Funny? I can do funny.
—But ...
She did not want to cause a *p-p*-problem, no, she didn't, but just one change, really, if they could, it *m*-muh-mattered ...
All right. Okay.
Second billing: Marilyn Monroe.
Cast as a secretary named Lois Laurel.

1953

Gentlemen Prefer Blondes.
Starring Jane Russell and Marilyn Monroe.
How to Marry a Millionaire.
Starring Marilyn Monroe, Betty Grable, and Lauren Bacall.
She was a big star.
A very big star.

January 14, 1954

Marilyn Monroe married Joe DiMaggio. "Joltin' Joe." "The Yankee Clipper." Hemingway called him "The Great DiMaggio" and "The Dago." She called him "My slugger." Three-time MVP winner. Thirteen-time All-Star.

Helluva ballplayer.

Joe DiMaggio was shy. He didn't say much. Did not like the celebrity spotlight. Except when he wasn't in it.

Didn't like his wife in it.

He thought she should come with him to San Francisco. Learn to cook linguini with a nice clam sauce. Cannelloni. Braciole like Mama Rosalie. Have a bunch of kids.

She thought she should star in a movie called *The Seven Year Itch.*

New York. Publicity shot. Police keep the crowd behind barricades. Marilyn Monroe on the subway grating at Lexington and 51st. Wind machine kicks in. Her skirt billows up.

> *I see London.*
> *I see France.*
> *I see Marilyn Monroe's underpants.*

And a whole! lot! more!

> *I see London.*
> *I see France.*
> *I see Marilyn Monroe's whosis!*

Joe DiMaggio has a problem with this aspect of moviemaking.

Restaurateur and long-time friend Toots Shor explains it to him: —Giuseppe, What do you want? She's just a goddamn dumb whore.

The marriage lasts 276 days.

August 4, 1962
Marilyn Monroe's bedroom
Los Angeles

Marilyn Monroe is dying.

Drugs are taking a long time to kill her.

Or perhaps, even with no audience, Marilyn Monroe is working the drama of it all.

Light gathers, phosphorescent waves all about her.

———

She wants to be smart.

She wants people to think she is smart.

She wants to think she is smart.

(Let's hear it for the only girl Blackbird!)

She wants to act.

Chekhov. Dostoyevsky.

A review: *In the demanding role of Grushenka, Marilyn Monroe exhibits what noted theater critic and raconteur Groucho*

Marx has acclaimed nothing less than 'a million dollar ass.'
She wants to be praised.
She wants to be loved.

June 29, 1956

She married Arthur Miller. Playwright. *All My Sons. Death of a Salesman. The Crucible.* A talent. An intellect. We've got a Tony Award for Best Author, the New York Drama Circle Critics' Award, and the Pulitzer Prize for Drama. Howzat? You want better? Check with his mother, Augusta ... Gussie: —*Oy*, even when he was just a *pisherke*, what a *kopf* he had!

House Unamerican Activities Committee comes after Arthur Miller. Pinko stuff in his plays. Hangs out with Commies. He wears glasses. Come on, I gotta spell it out? He's a Hebe!

Marilyn Monroe saves Arthur Miller's bacon—you should pardon the expression. Arthur Miller is married to Golden Dreams, for cryin' out loud. Not the girl next door, but the kinda sweet, kinda daffy, impossibly sexy roundheels you wished lived next door. How much more American can you get?

Miller, aw, he's okay. Don't bust his chops. Let him cop a walk.

Marilyn Monroe calls Arthur Miller *Pops*.

Arthur Miller introduces her to the work of many writers.

She writes poetry. Sad dolls. Weeping willows. Staircase men. Balloons. Jean Harlow.

She is scared to show Arthur her poetry. She doesn't want to hear that sniffy nose thing he does.

She discovers Edgar Lee Masters. She loves *Spoon River Anthology*.

Late in the evening, the hi-fi playing Respighi's *The Pines of Rome*, she's had enough to drink (1953 Dom Pérignon), and so she reads a few lines of Masters to Arthur Miller.

> *Immortality is not a gift, Immortality is an achievement; And only those who strive mightily shall possess it.*

Arthur Miller shakes his head. —Drivel, he says. —The quintessence of pulp-pap passing as profundity. Edgar Guest with a college sophomore's vocabulary and keen intellectual grasp. It is not impossible that *everything* that is wrong with America is contained in those resoundingly *dreadful* lines.

She finds the courage. —I ... I luh-like ...

—Of course, says Arthur Miller.

Shortly thereafter, she finds the journal he has accidentally left open on her dressing table.

> ... such a dumb *shiksa, takeh a goyishe kopf.* I do feel pity for her, but perhaps not love. And, selfish though it may be, I wonder what deleterious effects she might have on my *own* career ...

The Millers' marriage, uh, not in great shape.

He wrote a screenplay called *The Misfits.*

—Just for you.

Her role: A depressed divorced dancer, desperate for approval, acceptance, love.

She is NEED come a'walkin'—with a great body!

John Huston directed the film.

Clark Gable co-starred.

It was Gable's last film.

The film wrapped. Two days later, massive heart attack.

Clark Gable died ten days later.

Marilyn Monroe divorced Arthur Miller on January 20, 1961.

> "My life suddenly seemed as wrong and unbearable to me as it had in the days of my early despairs."
> – Marilyn Monroe

Tried to kill herself.

Did not.

Alcohol. Drugs. Psychiatry.

The Trinity for the Salvation of the Twentieth Century Soul.

Bangs President Jack Kennedy.

Who didn't?

Alcohol. Drugs. Psychiatry.

Tried to kill herself.

Did not.

Moved into modest house she'd bought in Brentwood, Los Angeles.

⸺❦⸺

"I was the kind of girl they found dead in a hall bedroom with an empty bottle of sleeping pills in her hand."
— Marilyn Monroe

Nembutal.
Chloral hydrate.
Vodka.

August 4, 1962
Marilyn Monroe's bedroom
Los Angeles

Marilyn Monroe
A corpse

For a moment
An aura

Norma Jeane walks
into the theate

Becomes
Light

⸺❦⸺

"Marilyn, being Marilyn, did what she always seemed to do: she absorbed all the available light and made it her own."
— Yona Zeldis McDonough, Editor,
All The Available Light: A Marilyn Monroe Reader

The main thing about being a hero
is to know when to die.
– Will Rogers

ABOUT THE AUTHOR

MORT CASTLE. A former stage hypnotist, folksinger, and high school teacher, Mort Castle has been a publishing writer since 1967, with hundreds of stories, articles, comics and books published in a dozen languages. Castle has won three Bram Stoker Awards®, two Black Quill awards, the Golden Bot (Wired Magazine), and has been nominated for The Audie, The Shirley Jackson award, the International Horror Guild award and the Pushcart Prize. In 2000, the Chicago Sun-Times News Group cited him as one of "Twenty-One Leaders in the Arts in Chicago's Southland." *Knowing When to Die* was a semi-finalist in the 2016 Leapfrog Press Fiction Contest. In a special Halloween issue scheduled for October of this year, Poland's Playboy Magazine will re-introduce fiction to its pages with Castle's story "Light," published in this collection. Castle and his wife, Jane, have been married forty-seven years and live in Crete, Illinois.

ॐ

ACKNOWLEDGEMENTS

"I Am Your Need" first published in *Brainbox II: Son of Brainbox*, edited by Steve Eller, Irrational Press (2001)

"The Doctor, The Kid, and The Ghosts in the Lake," published in *F Magazine 9*, edited by John Schultz (2009)

"Guidance" first published in *The Burning Maiden*, edited by Greg Kishbaugh & A.N. Ommus, Evileye Books (2012)

"Robot" first published in *You, Human: An Anthology of Dark Science Fiction*, edited by Michael Bailey, Dark Regions Press (2016)

"The Story Of Albert Glucklich" or **"What They Had In Common"** first published in *Brothers in Arms*, edited by Barry Hoffman, Gauntlet Press (2016)

"The Counselor" first appeared online at *Horror World*, edited by Nanci Kalanta (2011)

"The Oval Portrait" first published in *3Elements Review*, edited by Mikaela Shea Fowler (2015)

"Dreaming Robot Monster" first published in *Mighty Unclean*, edited by Bill Breedlove, Dark Arts Books (2012)

"Prayer" first published in *Chiral Mad 3*, edited by Michael Bailey, Written Backwards (2016)

"The Old Man and the Dead" first published in *Still Dead*, edited by John Skipp & Craig Spector, Signet Books (1992)

"Light" first published in *Shadow Show: All New Stories in Celebration of Ray Bradbury*, edited by Sam Weller & Mort Castle, William Morrow (2012)

PRAISE FOR KNOWING WHEN TO DIE

"What's that sound? Death knocking at the door. In Mort Castle's rich and varied collection of stories, death—by suicide and murder—comes knocking repeatedly, never in the same guise but always insistently, for Marilyn Monroe, Ernest Hemingway, and other mythic figures as well as for those not so famous: two opposing soldiers lying wounded in a trench, a couple grinding toward an unlivable old age, a school counselor to a suicide, and others perhaps not unlike ourselves. Castle's masterful storytelling reminds us that death will come knocking for all of us sooner or later, but rather than turn suicidal, we may find solace, challenge, and high entertainment in wonderful works of imagination such as Knowing When to Die, truly an unforgettable read."

——**Randy Albers**, Chair Emeritus, Fiction Writing,
Columbia College Chicago

"In Knowing When to Die Mort Castle serves up some of his finest nightmares yet; dark fantasy, suspense, and outright horror as only a master can."

——**Brian Augustyn**, comic book writer of *Gotham in Gaslight*

"Chilling, smart, big-hearted and crackling with Castle's signature razor-sharp prose, Knowing When to Die is the genre-bending showcase of a writer who can do it all, and who proves it on every page. Some of these stories are eerie, some lean toward the literary. Some are at turns bittersweet and laugh-out-loud hilarious, and many are all of the above. He explores the poignant subjects of youth, aging, loss, grief and guilt through a lens of the macabre, even diving into the American mythos of legendary figures like Ernest Hemingway and Marilyn Monroe, shattering the mirror of nostalgia in such a way that it reflects on our own troubled times and that stubborn persistence of that all too human condition of mortality. Mort Castle is one of the few writers anywhere who can turn the subject of death and dying

into a poignant, irreverent and exhilarating read."
   —**David Baker**, author of *Vintage*

"Elegant, elegiac, electrifying, enduring... Mort Castle's stories sneak up on you, tap you on the shoulder, and when you turn around...   WHAM!   The   emotional   wallop   is extraordinary. Working in hybrid corners of fantasy, science fiction, and horror, but always examining that shaggy dog known as the Human Condition, Mr. Castle is a truth teller, and belongs in the pantheon with Borges, Bradbury, and Gaiman."
   —**Jay Bonansinga**, *New York Times* bestselling author of *The Walking Dead: Return to Woodbury* and *Self Storage*

"Mort Castle is a genre unto himself. His work is — in the dictionary sense — singular in the horror field. If I had any control over the Fates, Knowing When To Die would signal a sea-change in the field, and one for the better. Castle's characters are the lost, the lonely, the discarded, the sinful, and those seeking some form of redemption. His stories are literate, moving, often hideously uncomfortable, and ultimately unforgettable. To read this collection is to witness a master storyteller at the height of his considerable powers. This is one of the most extraordinary collections I have ever had the privilege of reading. These stories will disturb you long after you've finished reading them."
   —**Gary A. Braunbeck**, Seven time recipient of the Bram Stoker Award and the author of *To Each Their Darkness*

"Mort Castle turns horror into a lyrical art form. Be very certain you're ready to experience darkness before diving into this tome."
   —**Eric S Brown**, author of *Bigfoot War* and *Casper Alamo*

"Mort Castle never ceases to amaze. He can still teach Stephen King a thing or two."
   —**David Campiti**, Co-Creator, *Warlords of Oz* and *Ex-Mutants*; Co-Founder of Innovation Publishing

"Mort Castle is a writer with a dark, spectacular imagination. In Knowing When To Die, he leads us through a number of dark doorways to places beautiful, and terrifying, and mordantly funny. This collection finds Castle at the height of his powers."

—**Bri Cavallaro**, *New York Times* bestselling author of *A Study in Charlotte*

"Mort Castle's stories pull us into startling and vividly specific worlds, but they also have a timelessness to them, an intimation of myth that touches the back of your neck. He's one of the greats."

—**Dan Chaon**, author of *Ill Will*, named one of the best books of the year by The New York Times

"In Knowing When to Die, Mort Castle presents an extraordinary kaleidoscope of characters, themes, and ideas. His style in many of these pieces resembles a kind of literary Cubism, with fragments of narrative—real, unreal, surreal—clashing and crashing against each other in unpredictable ways that somehow lead to dazzling new illuminations. If you're searching for a collection of standardized stories featuring the usual tired tropes of horror and fantasy fiction, then you'll have to look elsewhere. But if you'd like to know what happened the time Ernest Hemingway went to meet Edgar Allan Poe III, or experience a wild high-literary riff on the notorious 1950s Z-film Robot Monster, or see the world through the fractured mind and soul of perhaps the most vividly rendered Marilyn Monroe any author has yet given us, then Knowing When to Die is your book, and the brilliant Mort Castle is your writer."

—**Christopher Conlon**, Bram Stoker Award-winning editor of *He Is Legend: Stories Celebrating Richard Matheson*

"These are haunting, funny, unpredictable, and wildly imaginative stories that propel the reader through sometimes familiar landscapes but with eerie twists on our expectations. Mort Castle is the real deal!"

—**Ron Hansen**, author of *The Assassination of Jesse James by the Coward Robert Ford*, Pen/Faulkner Award Finalist

"Mort Castle's Knowing When To Die is brilliant. I smiled often, choked up occasionally, and relished every second of the ride. Taken together the stories form a kaleidoscopic quilt that while digging into the small spaces between individual life and death

somehow also tells the tale of the past American century as a whole. Mort not only aims for the stars, he surpasses them. Bravo!"
 —**David Lawrence**, Co-Creator *Ex-Mutants* and *New York Times* bestselling graphic novelist

"Buy this book. It is unforgettable. Mort Castle is one of the best storytellers of our time."
 —**J. Lehman**. Founder of the Cambridge Humanities Council, *LitNoir* and *Rosebud* magazines; Midwest Poet Laureate.

"In a time when some want to cast doubt upon fact, comes this courageous story collection, Knowing When to Die. Mort Castle, with wit and precision, bravely takes on the reality of our living and the exits we all must make. These are stories to keep you up at night—not for their horror, but for the truth they tell."
 —**Lee Martin**, author of *The Bright Forever*, Pulitzer Prize Finalist

"Mort Castle's compelling imagination always takes the reader to interesting places. Some are frightening, some beautiful, some happy and some sad, but all are insightful and keen to the human condition. This excellent collection should be on every midnight traveler's list of destinations."
 —**Robert McCammon**, *New York Times* bestselling author, *Boy's Life; Mine; Usher's Passing; The Listener*

"Knowing When to Die is a powerful, impossible-to-dismiss collection of stories, compelling in their range, tone, and form, spanning genres, eras, and worlds. Mr. Castle's writing is inventive, suspenseful, and darkly magical. Poetic and masterful, this is a one of a kind, bravura performance."
 —**Joe Meno,** author and playwright, winner of The Nelson Algren Fiction Award, *The Great Perhaps; Marvel and a Wonder*
"When Mort Castle writes, Rod Serling and Shirley Jackson look down from the stars and nod approvingly. From a meditation in the voice of the doomed Marilyn Monroe to a macabre little adagio about a counselor who really knows how to "set things right," Castle's tales are so sweet and sad and scary that the

reader can do nothing but hold on tight and repeat, they're only stories, they're only stories ..."

—**Jacquelyn Mitchard**, author, *The Deep End of the Ocean*, inaugural selection of Oprah's Book Club

"*Mort Castle has spent the last few decades quietly establishing himself as one of the finest writers of his generation of Baby Boomer scribes. His stories are fearless in their stylistic variations, informed by their literary acknowledgments, and laser-focused in their intention to make us think and feel in the most disturbing of ways.*"

—**Thomas F. Monteleone**, *New York Times* bestselling author

"*Mort Castle's Knowing When To Die is a fascinating, excellently crafted ... must-read...*"

—**Joe Pantoliano**, *New York Times* bestselling author and Emmy award winning "Best Supporting Actor" for *The Sopranos*

"*Mort Castle is one of our most literate practitioners of horror, a living master of the field, and he reinforces his status with Knowing When to Die. The tales collected herein are told in Castle's singular voice, infused with bittersweet humor, steeped in the heartache that comes in the quiet between beats. Tales told by ghosts, who in death perhaps have the clearest perspective on human life. Ghosts inspired by Marilyn Monroe and Ernest Hemingway and by you and me. As a writer, I feel enriched when I experience Castle's work. As reader, you will, too.*"

—**Jeffrey Thomas**, author of *Punktown*

"*The stories of Mort Castle's KNOWING WHEN TO DIE are clever, sharp meditations on mortality that evoke fear, melancholy, and wonder. I couldn't help but feel uplifted when I finished. This book is a dirge to celebrate.*"

—**Paul Tremblay**, author of *A Head Full of Ghosts* and *The Cabin at the End of the World*

"*In the exalted pantheon of great literary horror writers, Mort Castle stands among the very best. Knowing When To Die shows us why. Unsettling, melancholy, gripping and awash in dark imagination, the stories reveal Castle as a magician performing his greatest act yet of legerdemain."*

—**Sam Weller**, Two-time Bram Stoker Award winner and authorized Ray Bradbury biographer

"Yes, I'm stealing a simile, but a story collection from Mort Castle truly is like a box of chocolates. Every piece is tasty and wonderful in its own way, and has you reaching immediately for another. Knowing When to Die is a perfect example."

—**F. Paul Wilson**, *New York Times* bestselling author, *The Keep; Repairman Jack*

FORTHCOMING BOOKS

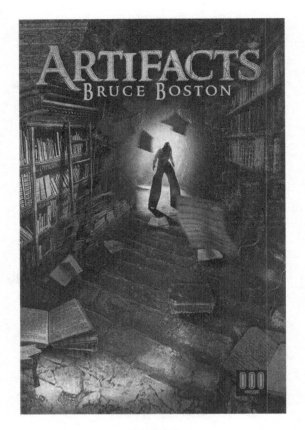

ARTIFACTS
by Bruce Boston
Petry Collection – **Paperback and eBook Edition**
July 2018

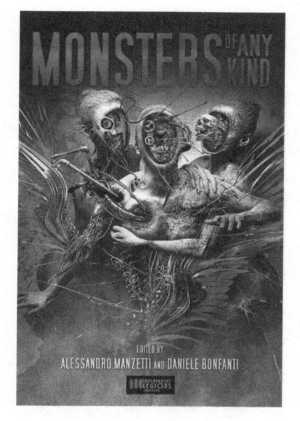

MONSTERS OF ANY KIND
Edited by Alessandro Manzetti and Daniele Bonfanti
Stories by: David J. Schow, Ramsey Campbell, Jonathan Maberry, Edward Lee,
Cody Goodfellow and many others
Anthology – **Paperback and eBook Edition**
September 2018

DARK MARY
by Paolo Di Orazio
Novel – **Paperback and eBook Edition**
October 2018

AVAILABLE BOOKS

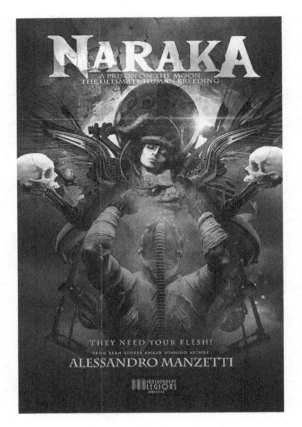

NARAKA
by Alessandro Manzetti
Novel – **Paperback and eBook Edition**
May 2018

A WINTER SLEEP
by Greg F. Gifune
Novel – **Paperback and eBook Edition**
April 2018

SPREE AND OTHER STORIES
by Lucy Taylor
Collection – **Paperback and eBook Edition**
February 2018

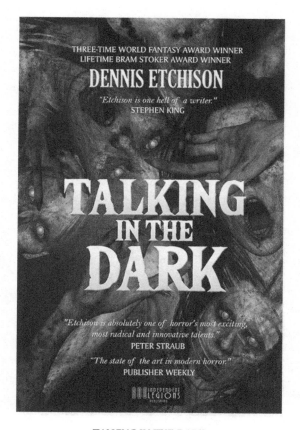

TALKING IN THE DARK
by Dennis Etchison
Collection – **eBook Edition**
December 2017

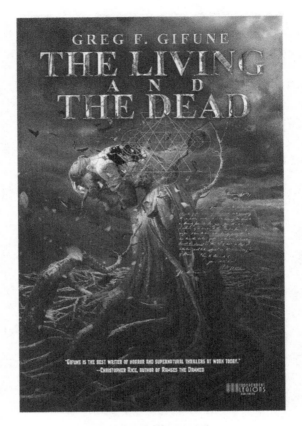

THE LIVING AND THE DEAD
by Greg F. Gifune
Novel – **Paperback and eBook Edition**
December 2017

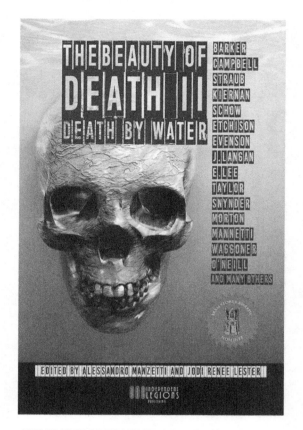

THE BEAUTY OF DEATH VOL. 2 - DEATH BY WATER
Edited by Alessandro Manzetti and Jodi Renée Lester
Anthology – **Paperback and eBook Edition**
November 2017

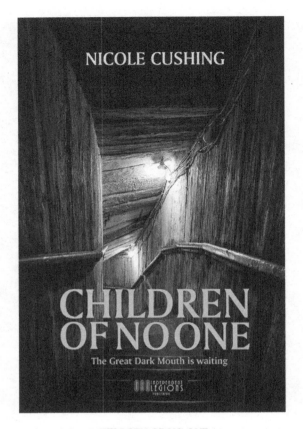

CHILDREN OF NO ONE
by Nicole Cushing
Novella – **Paperback and eBook Edition**
October 2017

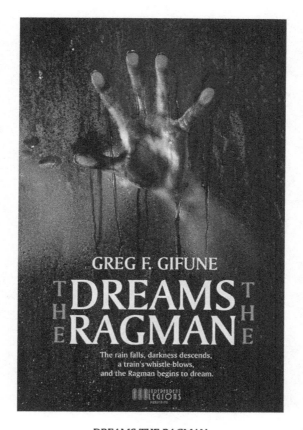

DREAMS THE RAGMAN
by Dennis Etchison
Novella – **eBook Edition**
October 2017

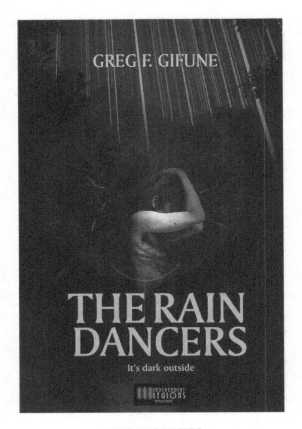

THE RAIN DANCERS
by Greg F. Gifune
Novella – **eBook Edition**
September 2017

THE WISH MECHANICS
by Daniel Braum
Collection – **Paperback and eBook Edition**
July 2017

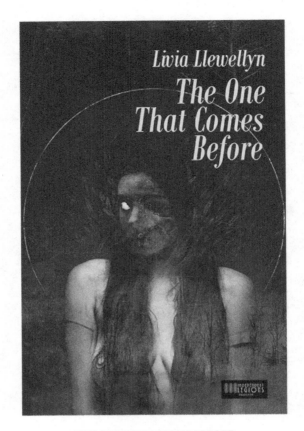

THE ONE THAT COMES BEFORE
by Livia Llewellyn
Novella – **Paperback and eBook Edition**
May 2017

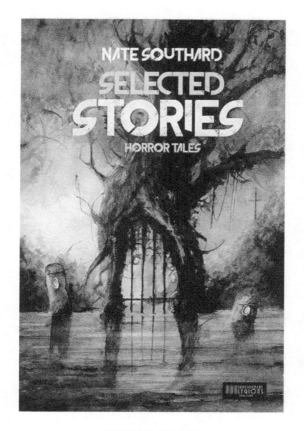

SELECTED STORIES
by Nate Southard
Collection – **Paperback and eBook Edition**
April 2017

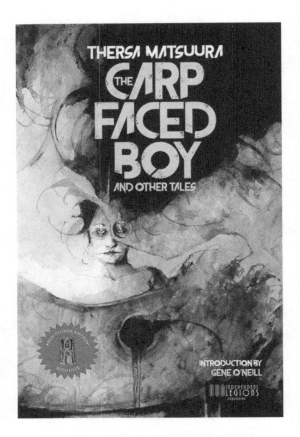

THE CARP-FACED BOY AND OTHER TALES
by Thersa Matsuura
Collection – **Paperback and eBook Edition**
February 2017

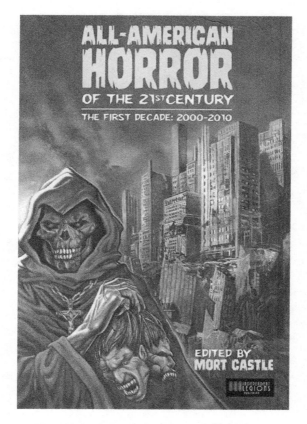

ALL-AMERICAN HORROR OF THE 21ST CENTURY
Edited by MortCastle
Anthology – **Paperback and eBook Edition**
November 2016

BENEATH THE NIGHT
by Greg F. Gifune
Novel & Novella – **Paperback Edition**
October 2016

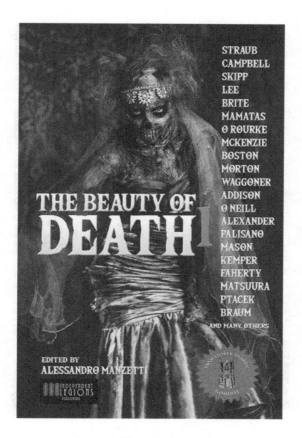

THE BEAUTY OF DEATH VOL 1
Edited by Alessandro Manzetti
Anthology – **eBook Edition**
July 2016

DOCTOR BRITE
by Poppy Z. Brite
Collection – **eBook Edition**
January 2017

WHAT WE FOUND IN THE WOODS
by Shane McKenzie
Collection – **eBook Edition**
September 2016

USED STORIES
by Poppy Z. Brite
Collection – **eBook Edition**
June 2016

THE HORROR SHOW
by Poppy Z. Brite
Collection – **eBook Edition**
August 2016

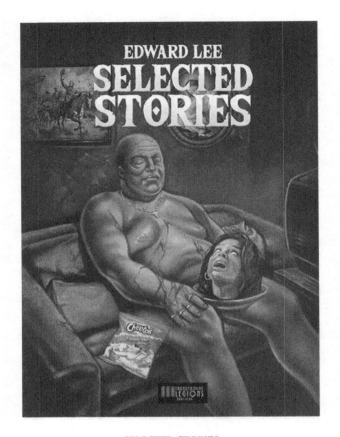

SELECTED STORIES
by Edward Lee
Collection – **eBook Edition**
July 2016

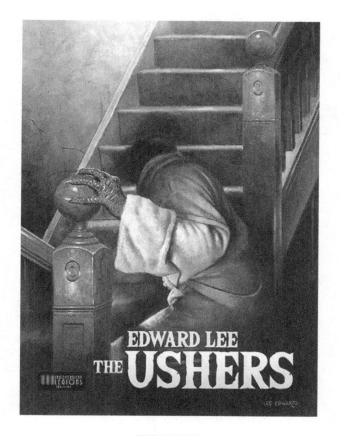

THE USHERS
by Edward Lee
Collection – **eBook Edition**
May 2016

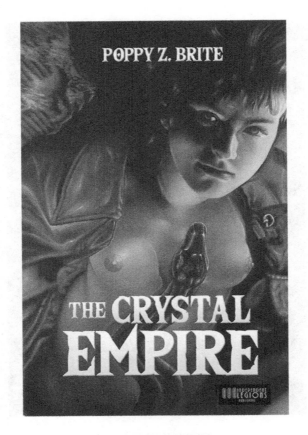

THE CRYSTAL EMPIRE
by Poppy Z. Brite
Novella – **eBook Edition**
May 2016

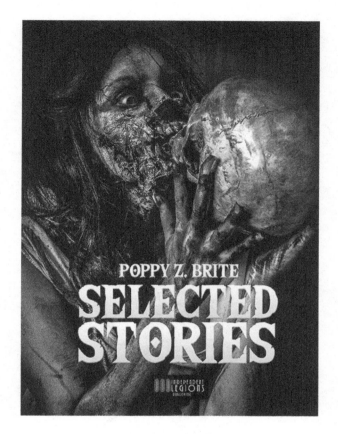

SELECTED STORIES
by Poppy Z. Brite
Collection – **eBook Edition**
February 2016

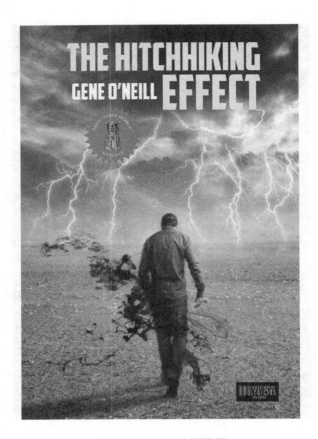

THE HITCHHIKING EFFECT
by Gene O'Neill
Collection – **eBook Edition**
February 2016

SONGS FOR THE LOST
by Alexander Zelenyj
Collection – **eBook Edition**
April 2016

INDEPENDENT LEGIONS PUBLISHING
by Alessandro Manzetti
Via Virgilio, 10 - 34134 Trieste (Italy)
+39 040 9776602

www.independentlegions.com
www.facebook.com/independentlegions
independent.legions@aol.com

Books in Italian:
www.independentlegions.com/pubblicazioni.html

SPECIALTY PRESS AWARD RECIPIENT

Made in the USA
Monee, IL
04 June 2024